IN DR DARLING'S CARE

BY
MARION LENNOX

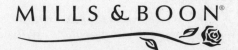

MILLS & BOON®

First published in Great Britain 2004
Large Print edition 2004
Harlequin Mills & Boon Limited,
Eton House, 18-24 Paradise Road,
Richmond, Surrey TW9 1SR

© Marion Lennox 2004

ISBN 0 263 18175 8

Set in Times Roman 16 on 17 pt.
17-1204-53291

Printed and bound in Great Britain
by Antony Rowe Ltd, Chippenham, Wiltshire

CHAPTER ONE

Memo:

Tell Emily: Doctors are not trained to tie pew ribbons.

Tell Emily: Doctors should not even need to admire pew ribbons. It's not written in the wedding contract. Is it?

Remember to admire the bridesmaids. Don't tell anyone I detest pink chiffon.

Do not slug Mrs Smythe when she asks me yet again when we can expect the patter of tiny feet.

Run. Run until I forget how many people are intending to watch me get married to-morrow...

SHE'D hit him.

Dear God, she'd hit him. Dr Lizzie Darling pushed Phoebe aside and shoved open the car door, her heart sprawled somewhere around her boots.

Where was he? There. Oh, no...

The man was face down in the mud right beside her car. Lizzie hadn't been going fast—this was a blind bend on an unmade road and it was raining. She'd crawled around the bend, but Phoebe had snapped her dog-belt at just the wrong time. The vast basset hound had launched herself joyously at her new mistress and Lizzie had been momentarily distracted. Or maybe distracted was too mild a description for the sensation of a basset tongue slurping straight down your forehead.

Whatever.

What had she done?

He must have been jogging, but what was someone doing jogging in this wilderness? He was in his late twenties or early thirties, Lizzie guessed. She'd reached him now. The sick dread in her heart was almost overwhelming. What damage had she caused?

Stay calm, she told herself. Look. Think. Triage. Sort priorities. And the first priority had to be to get herself calm enough to be professional.

Was he an athlete? With this build he surely could be. He was wearing shorts. His too-small T-shirt revealed every muscle. On his feet were running shoes, and he wore nothing else. Lying in the mud, he looked like some discarded Rodin sculpture. A wounded Rodin sculpture.

But...not dead? Please?

How hard had she hit him? She'd practically crawled around the blind bend. He must have run into her as much as she'd run into him.

She knelt in the mud beside him and put a hand to the side of his neck. Beneath her fingers his pulse beat strongly. That was good. There wasn't any blood. That was good, too.

But he wasn't moving. Why?

Her momentary calm was receding as panic built in waves. Lizzie might be a qualified medical practitioner but she was accustomed to her emergencies coming through the front entrance of her nicely equipped emergency department—not lying in the mud at her feet. She looked wildly around her, taking in her surroundings. She truly was in the middle of nowhere.

Birrini was a tiny fishing town on the south coast of Australia. The road through the forest into this town was one of the wildest in Australia. Scenic, they called it, but no tourists ever came here at this time of the year. Especially now, when the road surface had been ripped up for roadworks. Local traffic only, the sign had said, and for good reason. The road was a series of hairpin loops along a jagged coastline. On one side was a sheer cliff face; the other side dropped straight to the sea.

And what a sea! From here the ocean fifty feet down was a churning maelstrom of foam, with jagged shards of rock reaching up like suppliant fingers in the foam.

Suppliant fingers…hands raised in prayer. The analogy was a good one, she thought bitterly. Help was what she needed.

Action was what she needed. Here she was staring out to sea when she should be figuring out what to do with this guy.

She was figuring out how alone she was.

At least his breathing was fine. Her fingers had been moving over his face even as she looked about her, searching for what was most important. The stranger was face down but as her hand came over his mouth she felt the soft whisper of breathing. Thank God. She adjusted the position of his head a tiny bit—not enough to hurt if his neck was broken but a tiny sideways shift so his mouth and nose were clear of the mud.

So why wasn't he moving?

'What's wrong?' she whispered, but there was no answer.

Had he hit his head? He must have. Her fingers kept searching and found what they were seeking—an ugly haematoma on the side of his forehead. There was a little blood. Not much.

Maybe this was momentary. Maybe she'd just stunned him.

What else? She sat back, her trained eyes running over his body. What…?

His left leg.

She winced. It was all wrong. Just below the knee it twisted and was lying at a grotesque angle. She moved so that she was kneeling by it and winced again.

He'd snapped the bones beneath the knee. The tibia and the fibula must both be broken. She stared at it—at the position it was lying in. The position meant that there was a huge risk it'd be cutting off blood circulation. In fact…With fingers that felt numbed—horror had made her whole body seem numb—she edged off one of the guy's shoes and stared down. There was no mistaking the blue-white tinge to his toes.

No blood. She winced again, her mind racing. She was a good five miles out of Birrini. The way those toes had lost colour… Maybe he'd torn an artery.

No. Probably not. There didn't seem enough swelling to indicate that level of internal bleeding. But the blood vessels must be kinked, and the speed at which his foot had lost colour told her that he'd lose his leg before she could get help.

He needed X-rays, she told herself frantically. He needed careful manipulation under anaesthetic.

He had Lizzie and nothing and nowhere.

But at least she knew what had to be done, and as for anaesthetic...well, he was stunned now. He was temporarily—hopefully temporarily—out of it. What she needed to do would have him screaming in agony if he was conscious. She had morphine in the car but even so... It'd be far better to do this while he was unconscious and worry about pain relief if—when—he came around. So... 'Move, Lizzie,' she told herself. Any minute now he could gain consciousness and she'd have lost her chance.

But if only she had X-rays. She gave one last despairing glance at the road ahead. Nothing. She looked up at the cliff and then down to the sea below. There was nothing there to help her either.

She took a deep breath, then moved so that she was kneeling beside the leg. Another breath. She stared down, figuring out which way she should move. She might well do more damage with this manoeuvre—without X-rays she was flying blind. But the choice was to do nothing and watch his leg die, or try to move it into position. No choice at all.

She took hold of his left ankle in one hand and his knee in the other. It was harder than she'd thought. She was applying manual traction, easing the leg lengthwise and to the side. Trying—slowly and gently but still with strength—to move it.

It wouldn't go.

She wasn't brave enough. She had to be. More traction. She pulled and it moved. Just.

More traction. Twist…

And she heard it. Crepitus. The grating sound that fractured bones made as they moved against each other. Crepitus was an awful name for an awful sound but now she almost welcomed it.

Had she done it?

Maybe.

Her fingers were on his leg and she felt—she was sure she felt—the pulse return. She stared down, willing the colour to change. And in moments she was sure she wasn't imagining it. There was a definite improvement in the skin tone of the toes.

The man stirred and groaned. Little wonder. If someone had done to her what she'd just done to him, she'd have screamed so hard she'd have been heard back in Melbourne.

'Don't try and move,' she said urgently, her voice unsteady—but he didn't respond.

'Can you hear me?'

Nothing.

OK. What next? She'd saved him from a dead leg. Well done, Lizzie. Now she just had to save him from cerebral haemorrhage, or internal bleeding, or by being run over by another car as he lay in the road.

Her thoughts were cut off by another moan. The guy stirred and moaned some more and then shifted. He was finally coming round.

'You mustn't move,' she said again, and he appeared to think about it.

'Why not?' His voice was a faint slur but it sounded good to her. Not only was he gaining consciousness, he was gaining sense.

'You've been hit by a car.' She moved again so that she could see his face, stooping so her nose was parallel to his. 'You've broken your leg.'

He thought about that for a while longer. She'd laid her face in the mud beside his so that he could see her and she could see one of his eyes. She knew that he'd desperately need human contact and reassurance but she daren't move him further.

It was a crazy position to be in, but panic could make him move. He mustn't panic. So she lay in the mud so that he could focus.

He did. 'Whose car?' he managed, and she winced.

'My car.'

That was another cause for some long, hard thinking.

'My leg hurts,' he conceded at last. 'What else?'

'You tell me,' she said cautiously. 'Where else hurts?'

'My head.'

'I think you hit your head on the road.'

'How fast were you going?'

'Not fast at all,' she told him, a tiny bit of indignation entering her voice. He was making sense. No brain damage, then. 'You ran straight into me.'

'Yeah, like you were stopped and I just smashed into your car. You'll be suing me next.' Amazingly there was a hint of laughter in the man's voice. Laughter laced with pain.

But Lizzie wasn't up to laughter. Not yet. No brain damage, she was thinking. He had enough strength left to give her cheek. She found she was breathing again but she hadn't remembered stopping.

'I might sue you,' she said cautiously, still nose to nose with him in the mud. 'But not yet. I think we should consider scraping you off the road before we consult our lawyers.' She placed her hand on his head in a gesture of warmth and comfort. Strong as this man sounded, he was badly hurt and shock must be taking its toll. His hair was nice, she thought inconsequentially. Thick and wavy and deep, deep black. What she could see of his face was strong-boned and tanned. Her initial impression was really, really nice.

Which was a silly thing to think, given the circumstances. 'I'll get you something for the pain and ring for an ambulance,' she told him, and decided that shock was affecting her too. Her voice was decidedly wobbly. She couldn't make it sound efficient and clinical. Efficient and clinical was the last thing she felt like.

And his next words made her feel even less efficient. 'There's no phone reception out here,' the man muttered.

'No reception?'

'No.'

'But…' Leaving her hand resting on his head—he'd need touch, she knew—she rose and sat back on her heels and stared blankly down at him. 'But…why not?'

'Because we're in the middle of nowhere.' Stupid, he might have added, but he didn't. 'Why do you think I run out here?'

'Because *you're* stupid?' Lizzie whispered, trying to disguise her overwhelming sensation of sick dismay. No reception. Help!

'A man has to have peace some time.'

'Yeah, well, it should be really peaceful in hospital,' she snapped. This was a crazy conversation. He was lying face down in the road; she didn't even know what was wrong with him yet, and he was giving her cheek?

'Who said anything about hospital?'

'I did.' Her voice was starting to sound a bit desperate. She was feeling more out of control by the minute. 'That's where you're going.' She took a deep breath, searching for control. 'Now shut up while I examine you. And stay still!'

'Yes, ma'am.'

Silence. More silence. Lizzie started running her fingers over his body, searching for any lumps or bumps or obvious contusions. She could still only see his back but she was reluctant to roll him over. For a start that leg would hurt like hell. Second, if he'd hurt his back or his neck…

'I can wiggle my fingers and my left toes,' he told her. 'I'm not game to try my right toes.'

'I don't blame you. You've got a horrible break. I just had to straighten it to get circulation back.'

'Circulation...' He stirred and she placed a warning hand on his shoulder. 'Who the hell are you?'

'Lizzie Darling.' Her hands kept moving. One good thing about the scanty clothes he was wearing, her examination wasn't impeded. She put her hands under him and felt his ribs. His chest was broad and muscled and the ribs didn't seem damaged at all.

'Lizzie Darling.' He sounded bemused. 'Darling. As in not Lizzie Sweetheart but Lizzie Darling, daughter of Mr and Mrs Darling? Or wife of Mr Darling?'

She could afford to be magnanimous about her stupid name. Almost. If she hadn't been so fond of her mum and dad and her grandma she would have changed it years ago. But by deed poll. Not by marriage. 'Daughter will do,' she told him. 'That's the one.'

'You're the new locum, then?' he demanded, his voice incredulous, and she sat back and surveyed him some more. And worried some more.

She had more to concentrate on now than her entirely inappropriate name.

'I'll find something to splint that leg and then we'll try and roll you over.'

'But you are the doctor we're expecting?'

'I am.' She was searching the roadside. A branch had fallen from the cliff-top and it had crashed down, splintering into what she needed—a mass of wood of various lengths and thickness. Something here would do. She needed to roll him to check for further injuries but she wanted that leg immobile first.

At least the man was sensible. His voice was strong enough. With no blood, ease of breathing and fully conscious…she hadn't killed him and it didn't look like she was going to.

Locum. He'd said locum. He'd recognised her name?

'You knew I was coming?' She left him for a moment to think about it while she fetched her doctor's bag from the back of the car. Returning to kneel beside him, she located a syringe from the bag and fitted it with a morphine vial. By the time she had the needle ready, he had his answer ready. He might be conscious but he was still dazed.

'Yeah, I knew you were coming. Of course I did.'

'I'm just giving you something for the pain.'

'Morphine?'

'Mmm.'

'Five milligrams.'

'I thought ten,' she told him. 'I need to move you and it's going to hurt.'

'Five.'

'Hey, who's the doctor here?'

'I am,' he told her, and she paused, her syringe held to the light, and stared at the head in the mud.

'You?'

'Me,' he told her, his face still obscured. 'That's who you just ran over. Your boss. I'm Harry McKay, Birrini's doctor. You're here to replace me while I go on my honeymoon.'

Silence. She managed to finish checking the syringe but she was operating on automatic pilot. She couldn't focus on what he was saying and what was needed at the same time.

Medicine. Concentrate on medicine or she'd do something really stupid.

Seven and a half milligrams of morphine, she decided. When in doubt, compromise.

She swabbed his arm while he lay absolutely still. That fracture must be causing agony, she thought. He'd turned his head slightly and she could see the set look on his jaw.

Forget compromise. Forget he was a doctor. He was very definitely a patient. Ten milligrams of morphine whether he liked it or not.

She gave the dose subcutaneously, then moved down so she could work on his leg. She'd prepare the splint while she waited for the morphine to take hold.

'Five minutes tops before you get relief,' she told him.

'I know how long morphine takes to work.'

'I guess you do.' Her mind was racing. 'So…you're really the doctor I'm coming to replace?'

'I am.'

'You're getting married?'

'Yep.'

'Right.' She frowned. She shouldn't be talking to him like this. She should still be assessing him for shock. But it seemed he wanted to talk. To lie in the mud and think about what damage had been done… He'd be scared, she knew, but there was little reassurance she could give him until she could move him.

'There's no pain when you breathe?' she asked.

'No.'

'So no broken ribs?'

'Apparently not.'

She ran her hands down his spine again—
lightly. She wanted as much information as she
could before the morphine took hold. 'You can
feel that?'

'Yeah.'

'No loss of sensation?'

'No.'

'No pain in your back at all?'

'No. Only in my leg. And my head.'

'That's good.'

'Yeah. Fantastic.'

'Sorry.' She managed a smile. She moved up
and placed her hand over his, feeding him
warmth she thought he'd be desperate for. She
was wearing a light jacket but it was already
soaked and it held no warmth at all. She needed
a blanket. She always carried a blanket in her
own car, but this was a hire car. She was lucky
she had a medical bag. The bag had been pro-
vided by the locum service when she'd agreed
to take on this job, but there was no blanket and
he must be freezing.

'I'm as strong as a horse. I'll live,' he said
curtly, and she blinked.

'That's my job,' she said mildly. 'To decide
that.' But she smiled again and the tension eased
off a bit. Despite his attempt at humour, he was
gripping her hand as if he needed it.

'This is stupid. My face is in the mud. I'm going to try and sit up.'

'If you try and move before I splint your leg, your brain will be in orbit,' she told him. She relented a little. 'It mightn't be that bad, but your circulation was cut off. I don't want to risk the bones moving again.'

'Compound fracture?'

'Comminuted. The bones are right out of alignment but they haven't broken the skin.'

'That's lucky.' He tried to smile.

'Yeah.' He had courage. She'd have rolled herself off the edge of the cliff by now, she decided. The pain level in that leg would be dreadful.

And all she could do for the moment was wait. She sat on the road, holding his hand, forcing herself to stay still. To stay calm. The morphine would kick in soon and then she could work, but it wouldn't hurt to wait.

Phoebe was in the passenger seat of her car, staring out with the desperation of a basset who'd been abandoned by the world. Too bad. Phoebe had caused this mess. It wouldn't hurt her to wait either.

Her car was parked in the middle of the road, though. Maybe that was a problem.

'No one's likely to come.' Harry was obviously thinking as she was thinking. 'Not this way. Council's doing road work and the road's blocked at either end. That's why I'm running here. I knew the road would be deserted.' He thought about it a bit more and decided it didn't make sense. 'But it wasn't deserted. How did you get through? The only way through is via the hills—not along the coast road.'

'The coast road was open when I came last night.'

'You came last night?'

'I booked a holiday cottage half a mile south of here.'

'You're supposed to be staying at the hospital.'

This was one crazy conversation. He was trying to take his mind off the pain until the morphine kicked in, she decided. OK. The least she could do was help.

'I can't stay at the hospital. I have a dog. What do you think caused this accident?'

'You have a dog?'

'How's the pain level?'

'Horrible. Tell me about your dog.'

'Phoebe's stupid.' She touched his hand again, gave it a quick squeeze and then released it, aware as she did of a sharp stab of reluctance to let it go. This comfort business wasn't all one way, she thought ruefully. She'd had a sickening shock. She needed his presence as much as he needed hers. 'The morphine should have taken by now.'

'Not enough.'

She glanced at her watch and winced. It wasn't going to get any better than this. 'I need to splint your leg. How are you at biting bullets?'

'Do you have a supply of bullets?'

'Maybe not,' she conceded. 'I have a Mars Bar.'

'I'd throw up.'

'You're feeling nauseous?'

'Horribly.'

'Don't throw up until we get your face out of the mud,' she advised, but she had to move. She lifted her branch and laid it along the back of his leg. It was awful. Rolled up newspapers, the emergency manuals said. They were generally antiseptic and rigid enough to hold. So where were rolled-up newspapers when she needed them?

She was wearing a light jacket—cotton. Formal business. Not enough to give any warmth. But as padding for the splint, at least it'd stop him getting slivers of wood in his leg.

She hauled off her jacket and twisted it round the wood. She laid the makeshift splint along his leg and then carefully started winding bandage along its length. It was impossible to operate in these conditions without shifting his leg slightly and she was aware by the rigidity in his body how much she was hurting him.

'What sort of dog?' he muttered and she grimaced. There was real pain in his voice. Maybe ten milligrams of morphine wasn't enough.

'Basset.'

'Why do you have a stupid basset?'

'I inherited her.' He was using Phoebe to focus on something that wasn't pain and she could do the same. 'My grandma died three weeks ago. She left me Phoebe. I live in North Queensland. Phoebe's the human equivalent of eight months pregnant. I can't take her home until she's delivered the pups. It's hot up north and the heat would kill her, if she survived the journey. No kennel will take her this far into her pregnancy, and no airline will carry her, so I'm stuck here until the pups are born.'

Harry thought about that and bit on his imaginary bullet some more. 'That's why you applied to be my locum?'

'That's right.'

Now what? She had the splint in place now. The leg was fixed as rigidly as she could manage. The morphine would be working as well as it could.

It was time to move.

'You're sure no one's likely to come along this road?' she asked, and he grunted into the mud.

'Nope. We're on our own. It's time to turn me over and check my face hasn't fallen off.'

'Does it feel as if it has?'

'Nope, but this mud pack has done me all the good that it's going to do me. Let's go.'

Lizzie was very worried. If she had an ambulance here she'd have him moved immobile onto a fixed stretcher until she'd thoroughly checked that neck and spine. She couldn't leave him lying in the mud on the side of the road, though. For a start, if he lost consciousness again he could even drown. It was still raining, a steady drizzle that was making her cold to the bone. They'd both have hypothermia if she didn't move.

So, feeling as anxious as she'd ever felt in her entire medical career, she moved to his shoulders and put her face down in the mud again, nose to nose.

'I'm going to roll you over now,' she told him. 'Don't try to help me.'

'If I don't try to help you then you'll never do it,' he muttered. 'How tall are you?'

'I'm tall.'

'You don't sound tall.'

'I have a short voice.'

'I can see you sideways. You look really short.'

'From where you are I must look eight feet or so.' She put her hands under his shoulders. 'I'm sorry but your leg's going to hurt when I do this. But I want to roll you keeping your back and neck as rigid as possible.'

He forgot about the short bit. She could see him brace.

'OK. Let's give it a shot.'

In the end he rolled with ease. There couldn't be major damage, she decided with relief. He could use his still strong hips to roll himself as she supported his shoulders and neck.

'Slow,' she said urgently. 'Keep it slow.'

A minute later he was lying on his back, practising deep breathing as his leg settled. She took three deep breaths herself and met his gaze. Done. He was still breathing and breathing well. His hands were still moving. There clearly wasn't an unstable break in the vertebrae.

He was staring up at her with the bluest eyes...

They really were the most extraordinary eyes, she thought, stunned. Or maybe it was just the situation and the relief of having him look up at her with eyes that were lucid.

No. It wasn't just that. They really were the most extraordinary eyes. His face was mud-stained and etched with strain, the bruise on the side of his forehead was raw and ugly, but she could see laughter lines around his eyes. A wide generous mouth looked as if it was meant for smiling.

He was trying to smile now.

'S-see,' he said. 'No problem.' After a short pause he added, 'Maybe you could give me that extra five milligrams of morphine.'

'You've already had it.' She was checking his chest now, his shoulders, everything she could see of him. 'I'm sorry but that's all I can give you.'

'Damned managing woman.'

'That's what I'm famous for. Is it only your leg that hurts?'

'Isn't that enough?'

'I guess it is.'

'Tell me again why I employed you?'

'So you can get married.' She looked uneasily at the car. She was going to have to get him in there. Somehow.

'You can't lift me.'

'No.'

'But you can't leave me sprawled in the road for some other dingbat city doctor to run down.'

'How many dingbat city doctors do you have around here?'

'Ha,' he said in satisfaction. 'You admit it. Dingbat city doctor. That's an admission of guilt if ever I heard one. Where are witnesses when you need them?'

'There's always Phoebe.'

'Phoebe?'

'My basset.'

'Right. Your mother-to-be.'

'You know, if you just shut up for a minute I might be able to think of a plan.'

'Yeah?'

He was mocking her. 'Yeah,' she said, temporarily distracted. 'I might.'

'It's a hard call. You help me haul myself into your car or…or what?'

'I'll think of something.'

'Fine. Let's get me into the car first.'

'And if you've broken your back?'

'I haven't.'

'How do you know?'

'It's my back. I'd know.'

'Like you've got an X-ray machine.' Her panic must have shown through, because suddenly the roles changed. He reached out and grasped her hand.

'Lizzie, I don't have a broken back,' he told her in a voice that was suddenly stronger than hers was. 'You've splinted my leg. I have nerve endings tingling all over the place, which tells me I'm fine. But bruised. I'm feeling sleepy already, which will be the morphine taking effect. If you wait any longer the morphine is going to put me to sleep and there's no way a runt of a little thing like you can drag me unconscious into the car.'

'I'm not a runt of a thing.' She was running her spare hand along the side of his neck, checking, checking…

But he was staring up into her face, and he was still gripping her hand, and she was suddenly absurdly aware of how close they were. Which was ridiculous. She was a doctor. He was a patient.

'Lizzie…' His voice was starting to slur a little and his other hand came up and grasped her fingers. Which made her even more aware of his closeness. His maleness.

His…need?

'You can't do any more for me here in the mud,' he said softly. 'This is going to hurt me more than it is you.'

'I know. That's why—'

'Let's just do it and talk about it later.'

It was a nightmare. Her car was way too small. She reversed it so her rear car door was right beside him but every movement must have sent shards of pain shooting down his injured leg.

She saw his agony but there was nothing she could do about it. Somehow they managed to haul him up into a sitting position on the end of the back seat. Then she supported the leg as best she could while he dragged himself backwards right in. By the time he was safely in, his face was so drained of colour she was afraid he'd pass out.

'Just don't let the dog near me,' he muttered as she hauled the seat belt around him. Phoebe was in the front passenger seat, her great nose drooping over the back support as if she was incredibly concerned with all that was going on. And shocked. And sad.

That just about summed Phoebe up, Lizzie thought bitterly. Concerned, shocked and sad. That's what her eyes said, but in reality what was going on was a deep internal pondering as to when dinner could be expected to appear. As this deep pondering started approximately two seconds after she'd finished last night's dinner, it didn't leave much brain room for anything else.

'Phoebe won't jump on you,' Lizzie told him. 'She doesn't do jumping. I don't think she knows what it is. Are you OK?'

'No. I have a broken leg. Can I have some more morphine?'

'You know very well you can't.' She cast him a really worried glance. 'It must really hurt.'

'You're not supposed to say that,' he said faintly, and there was that amazing trace of laughter in those amazing eyes. 'It should be, ''Come on, lad, pull yourself together. You'll be right by morning. Take an aspirin and have a nice lie-down and give me a call…'' Are you sure I can't have any more morphine?'

'I'll get you to hospital and get you settled first.'

'So if I go into cardiac arrest you can resuscitate me.'

'That's the ticket.'

'Maybe I could just cardiac arrest for the next few minutes so I could pass out on the way.'

'I'm sure you don't mean that.' The seat belt clicked into place, but she was still leaning across him, staring worriedly into his face. 'I'll drive really, really carefully.' She took a deep breath and straightened away from him. 'Besides, you can't go into cardiac arrest. Don't you have a wedding to go to?'

'Tomorrow?'

'Maybe not.'

'Emily will have kittens.'

'Emily being your fiancée?'

'That's the one.'

'Well, she can have kittens and Phoebe will have puppies and they'll all live happily ever after. Meanwhile…I'm sorry, Dr McKay, but there's no easy way to do this. Let's get you to hospital.'

CHAPTER TWO

Memo:
I will not scream.
I will not panic.
I will not tell this crazy woman and her crazy dog to get out of my town this minute.
I will remember that I might just need them...

BY THE time they reached the tiny township hospital Harry was grey. His face was etched with pain and he was holding himself rigid. Lizzie steered her car into the entrance of the tiny emergency department, switched off the engine and put her hand on the hooter.

'Don't do that,' he told her. 'They'll think I'm an emergency.'

'You are an emergency.'

'I'm fine.'

Ha! She was past arguing. 'You might be fine, but I'm not,' she told him. 'I'm wrecked. Is the duty doctor here now or will he or she have to be called in?'

'Duty doctor?'

'Duty doctor.' She was suffering from reaction here. Why didn't a whole medical team burst from the doors, ready to take over?

'There's no duty doctor. There's only me, and I'm decidedly off duty.' Harry's voice was strained to breaking point and Lizzie stared at him in horror.

'What?'

'You heard.'

'You mean...' She caught her breath, appalled. 'You mean this is a one-horse town?'

'A one-doctor town. Yes. That's why I need a locum.'

'They didn't tell me it was a one-doctor town.' The doors were finally opening now, and a uniformed nurse was hurrying toward them. The nurse was eye-catchingly lovely, in her early thirties maybe, trim, and elegant and... well, just plain beautiful. Her long black hair was braided into a severe rope hanging over her shoulder almost to her waist. Her hair would be gorgeous unbraided, Lizzie thought inconsequentially. More gorgeous. The woman herself would be even more gorgeous if she didn't look so worried.

She wasn't the only one worrying. Lizzie was distracted enough not to be worrying about someone else's worry. She should be worried about the man on the back seat—she was—but she was also appalled at the thought of not having help.

'The people at the locum agency told me one of the doctors was getting married and needed a fill-in,' she said slowly, thinking it through. 'One of the doctors. Implying several.'

Harry closed his eyes, an unmistakable wash of pain sweeping through. 'If they said one of the doctors then they lied.'

'But... I would never have come if...' Her voice rose in panic. 'I don't do this. Not alone. I can't.'

'Welcome to Birrini, Dr Darling,' Harry muttered, his face grim. 'I think you'll find you can. It's amazing what you can do when you have no choice.' Then, as the nurse reached the car and pulled open the back door, he managed a strained smile. 'Hello, Emily. This is Dr Darling. Our locum. She's here to replace me. It was to be while you and I got married, but maybe now it's while she mends my broken leg.'

She couldn't worry about her lone status now. Like Harry said, she had no choice.

Once in the relative security of the hospital she turned on her autopilot. Never mind that she was soaked to the skin. Harry needed her more than she needed to take care of herself.

Medicine first, she told herself, and tried to stop the tremors sweeping through her body. Her spare clothes were back at the holiday cottage. She'd worn a smart little business suit into town to meet the medical community. The smart little business suit was now a bedraggled mess, with the jacket wrapped around Harry's splint. Lizzie's mass of bright blonde curls had been hauled into a neat businesslike knot when she'd set out that morning but that was a thing of the past, too. Her curls were now hanging in soaked tendrils around her face, mud-matted and coldly dripping.

It didn't matter. It couldn't matter.

At least Harry was being warmed. She could examine him now with considerably more care than her roadside check, and she did so as she and Emily stripped him and dried him and gently manoeuvred him into a hospital gown.

'I'm not wearing a hospital gown,' he muttered.

'Harry, stop being silly.' Emily's voice was laced with tears and Lizzie gave her a sharp glance. There wasn't a lot of professional detachment here—though maybe she was being unfair.

If someone brought my fiancé into town, squashed, maybe I'd be a bit tearful too, she told herself.

Maybe. She thought about Edward for a fraction of a second and grimaced. Come to think about it, there was a lot to be said for squashed fiancés.

'My pyjamas are just through in my quarters,' Harry was murmuring sleepily, and she forgot thinking about Edward and dredged up a smile.

'I can't get at you as easily in your pyjamas.'

'That's what I'm afraid of.'

Amazingly he was laughing. He was drifting in and out of sleep, on the edge of pain, but he could still smile. She wished he'd go completely to sleep. Indignity was the last thing he should be thinking of.

He did fade back into sleep as she and Emily prepared him for X-ray. She was grateful. Once again she had to move the leg slightly, straightening it a little more while she had the chance. The last thing she needed now was for that blood vessel to kink and block again.

The woman, Emily, worked by her side, but she worked in silence, her mouth a tight, grim line. Her tears had receded, but she still looked sick.

'He'll be OK,' Lizzie said gently, and Emily gave her a fierce, angry glance.

'You don't understand.'

No. She didn't. She couldn't understand anything but what was before her. She should probe, but she was too shocked and cold and numb herself to take it further.

Finally, with the analgesia working well, she took the X-rays she wanted. By this stage Harry's head wound was worrying her more than the leg. He'd lost consciousness back on the road. He was sleeping now. If he was bleeding internally...

'My headache's eased,' he muttered as she took the last film, and her eyes flew wide. She'd thought that he was asleep, and here he was reading her thoughts.

'I'm sorry?'

'I don't have a cracked skull.'

'I'm checking anyway, if you don't mind,' she told him, and he nodded and seemed to drift off again.

Good. The man made her nervous just by...just by being. And so did this silent nurse, hovering over her like a terrified parent.

Wasn't there anyone else in this hospital?

She couldn't mind. She just had to ignore them both and do what she thought right. Though she'd quite like someone to notice, a, that she was filthy and (more urgently), b, that she was freezing.

No one did, so neither did she. Or rather, she did notice. She just didn't turn into an ice cube and melt right there on the floor of the X-ray department. She didn't have time.

Finally someone noticed. Harry.

After his initial protest Harry had seemed content to leave everything in her hands, and Emily was still working on autopilot. But with the X-rays finished, Lizzie grasped the head of the trolley to push him back through to the ward and his hands reached out and grasped hers. He'd woken properly this time, and his hands had a strength she hadn't believed possible.

'You're still dripping.' He stared up at her in concern, his face right under hers. 'Lizzie, it's time you were warm and dry,' he managed, his words only slightly slurred. 'Emily, look after her.'

'We'll look after you first,' Emily told him. The woman seemed almost more shocked than Harry.

'Can I help?'

And here was the cavalry, in the form of a freckle-faced senior nurse standing in the doorway. She stared from Emily to Harry and then to Lizzie, and her eyes were wide with shock. 'Joe said there'd been an accident. Dr McKay!'

'Dr McKay's broken his leg,' Emily snapped, and the woman's eyes widened even further.

'Right. Goodness. I've just come on duty. What needs doing?'

'Emily will take me through to the ward,' Harry said strongly. 'May, can you look after Lizzie? Dr Darling.'

'Dr Darling?'

'That's me,' Lizzie said wearily. 'Lizzie Darling. The locum.' Locum? Even the word sounded wrong. She didn't feel like a locum. She was tired of being doctor in charge. If she didn't drop her bundle soon she'd fall straight over.

And the woman had the sense to see it. She focused and her eyes narrowed in concern.

'You're the basset hound's mum?'

'I'm the basset hound's mum.'

'This gets better and better.' The woman smiled a greeting and held out her hand. 'And our new doctor?'

'Mmm.' She was starting to shake uncontrollably and May felt it through their linked hands.

She looked uncertainly at Emily. 'Dr Darling's making a puddle on our nice clean floor,' she told her. 'Can I take her away and dry her off?'

'Do that,' Emily told her, distracted. 'Fine.'

'I'll show you where you can shower, Doctor, and if you like I'll find you some dry clothes.' May left no one room for a change of mind. She had Lizzie's arm and was leading her to the door. 'Or do you have some dry clothes in your car? Jim, our orderly, is looking after your dog. He found her in your car and took her out before she ripped the upholstery to shreds. I'll ask Jim to fetch your luggage, shall I?'

'My luggage is at a holiday cottage five miles south of here, but even a hospital gown's preferable to what I'm wearing now,' Lizzie managed, thankful all the same for the tiny realisation that she wasn't completely alone. Someone cared. But she wasn't ready to drop her bundle yet. Not completely. 'I'll check these X-rays first.'

'The X-rays will be fine,' Harry muttered from the trolley, and Lizzie nodded.

'Oh, right. Of course they will be. No break at all. And here I was imagining the bend in your leg.'

'Just stick a cast on it.'

He had no idea. Had he heard what she'd told him about fractures and circulation? About how close he'd been to losing the leg?

'You're going to look really odd tomorrow wearing a cast,' Emily whispered to him. She was practically wringing her hands and had been no help at all while the X-rays had been taken. It was all very well being shocked, Lizzie thought, but maybe she could be shocked later when she was no longer needed.

Lizzie intended being shocked later. Maybe now?

What had Emily said? *You're going to look really odd tomorrow wearing a cast.*

She was talking about their wedding as if it was still going to happen, Lizzie thought incredulously. But now wasn't the time to enlighten her. It wasn't the time to talk about weddings. Harry desperately needed to sleep, to let the painkillers take over. She needed to check his X-rays and then get her own head in order.

It wasn't the place for anything but making sure this man didn't have a cerebral bleed—and making herself stop this awful shivering.

'Can you take Dr McKay through to a ward and settle him?' she asked wearily. 'Harry, you need to sleep. I'll talk you through the results of the X-rays when you wake.'

But he was looking at her and there was real concern showing through the pain and weariness etched onto his face. 'Only if you promise to look after yourself,' he told her.

'I will.' She touched his hand, staring down at him and suddenly fighting a stupid urge to weep. 'Of course I will. Looking after me is what I'm principally good at. Now sleep.'

His head was fine. Lizzie checked the X-rays from every angle and could see no damage at all. It must have been a fair bang to make him lose consciousness but there was little to show for it now. She'd watch him carefully for signs of internal bleeding, but every sign was that he'd been lucky.

Not so the leg. Lizzie held the X-ray up to the screen and May whistled.

May had introduced herself with cheer. 'I'm May. I'm general dogsbody round here. Basic nurse training twenty years ago. All care and no responsibility. Emily's our nurse administrator but I guess with Emily in a flap I'm it.'

She was a welcome *it*. The freckle-faced forty-something woman exuded a warmth that Lizzie was in sore need of. Now she'd checked Harry's head she could concentrate on that hot shower and dry clothes.

'He's not going to be walking down any aisle tomorrow, is he?' May asked shrewdly, and Lizzie shook her head.

'No.' She looked again at the X-rays. She'd been very lucky to get the leg back into a position where the blood vessels weren't blocked. Very lucky.

'It'll need pinning?'

'It's a corkscrew break right through, with breaks in both tibia and fibula. He can do six weeks in traction and possibly end up with a really bad result or he can get it pinned. Plus, there are slivers of bone that need fixing or removing.'

'Can you pin it here?' May asked, and Lizzie shook her head.

'Heck, no. Pin this leg? Our Dr McKay needs an orthopaedic surgeon and an anaesthetist. Maybe I could do the anaesthetic but... How good are you at joining broken bits of bone together?'

May grinned and shook her head. 'Carpentry's never been my strong point.'

'Then we ship him out to someone who can.'

The nurse turned back to the screen and screwed up her nose. 'So the wedding's off?'

'Absolutely. I'd like him evacuated as soon as possible. Soon. His head looks good but he did lose consciousness for a bit. If there's the slightest chance of him having an intracranial bleed, he needs to have it somewhere near a neurosurgeon. He can go to Melbourne, see out his danger period in a nice city hospital with all the facilities, get his leg pinned and plated and then come back here and recuperate.'

'With you looking after him?'

Lizzie let her breath out in a long slow sigh. 'I guess.'

This wasn't the locum position she'd planned. Absolutely not. Once upon a time she'd been a family doctor—for two short years after she'd graduated. Now—after one awful day she hated even to think about—she was a nine-to-five doctor. She looked after the emergency department of a city hospital. She did her absolute best for everyone while she was on duty and then she walked away.

She closed shop.

And here, a tiny fishing village with its only doctor incapacitated... This place could suck her in, she thought fearfully. She should drive out of here right now. She could go back to the locum agency and tell them they were liars.

She'd get another job. There were always jobs for locums. But...

'We'll be in a mess without you,' May told her, and she winced.

'I'm like you,' she muttered. 'I'm all care, no responsibility.'

'Unless you're stuck,' May said shrewdly. 'And you are stuck. There's no one else. If Harry's away and you don't stay we'll have to close the hospital until he gets back. All those people…'

'How many?' Lizzie demanded, startled, and May gave an apologetic shrug.

'Well, five. Five in acute care. But there's a nursing home, too.'

'That wouldn't have to shut.'

'No, but the hospital would.'

Lizzie tried to get her tired mind to think. This wasn't right. Something wasn't right. 'Um… I only agreed to come last Tuesday. This wedding's obviously been planned for months.'

'We had another locum booked,' May told her. 'Only he realised how remote it was and pulled out.'

So that's why they'd lied to her. Lizzie's heart hardened. 'Then I can—'

'No, you can't,' May told her. 'You're nice.'

'I'm not nice.'

'Yeah, you are. I've seen your dog. Anyone who didn't get a dog like that put down at first sight has to be more than nice.'

'You mean really, really stupid,' Lizzie said, and May grinned.

'You said it, Dr Darling, not me. But if the cap fits...'

It was the best shower she'd ever had in her life. Lizzie stood under the hot water and let the heat and the steam soothe away the mud and the cold and the shock. Long after she was thoroughly clean she still stood there, letting the heat soothe her tired brain. Making her mind blank. Giving her time out.

Somewhere someone called Jim was looking after Phoebe. That in itself was a godsend. Ever since Grandma had died Phoebe had followed her like a shadow and Lizzie, who didn't do family, who didn't do connections, was finding it a weighty strain.

Phoebe was supposed to be back at the holiday cottage right now, but when Lizzie had shut the gate behind her this morning Phoebe had set up a wail that would have woken the dead. Then she'd launched herself at the wooden gate like a battering ram, over and over again, hurling her ungainly body at the wood in manic desperation to follow.

'You're pregnant,' Lizzie had told her. 'You'll go into premature labour if you don't stop it. I'll be back tonight.'

But Phoebe had kept right on howling and battering. Finally Lizzie had shoved her in the car. She was staying down here because of the dratted dog. If she had to do this locum job with Phoebe sprawled over her feet while she took surgery then the patients would just have to wear it.

What had May said? Anyone who hadn't had a dog like this put down at first sight had to be more than nice.

'Ha.'

She wasn't being nice. It was just... Just that she was stuck.

Phoebe had been Grandma's dog. Grandma had loved Phoebe and she'd loved Lizzie. Grandma had been the one constant in Lizzie's trauma-filled upbringing and the thought of losing her...

No. She wasn't going to cry. She blinked and splashed her face with some more hot water. She wouldn't cry. But neither could she put Phoebe down.

'But what on earth ever possessed you to let her get pregnant?' she wailed to her grandmother. 'One basset hound I can cope with.' She thought about it and changed her story. 'No. One basset hound I can survive. But a pregnant basset hound? A hound with puppies? And they mightn't even be bassets.'

Actually, that wasn't such a bad thought. Maybe they'd have their father's intelligence. Whoever the father was.

'Maybe he's a Border collie.

'Yeah? Border collies are smart. You seriously think a Border collie would look twice at our Phoebe?

'Maybe not.'

'Um…is there someone in the shower with you?' a voice called. 'If there's a party happening in there I'll go away. I don't want to disturb you.'

May. Whoops, Lizzie thought, and stuck her head out of the shower curtain to reply.

'I'm talking to the plughole,' she told her with an attempt at dignity, and May nodded.

'It's a good thing, too,' May said cautiously. 'I find they don't talk back.'

'This one was talking back something dreadful.'

'Dratted plughole. I'll call a plumber and have it fixed.'

This woman could be a friend, Lizzie thought gratefully, and the world looked brighter all of a sudden. Especially when she saw what May was holding.

'My clothes!'

'Jim drove out and brought your things in.'

Lizzie considered. 'All my things?'

'All your things. Including the dog basket.'

'Gee, that was nice of Jim.'

'You're dripping on the floor.'

'Hand me my towel,' Lizzie said without committing herself further until she'd had a little think about what was happening here. She retired behind the shower curtain and started towelling herself. And thinking.

'I can't stay here.'

'You have to stay here.'

'Why?'

'You're the only doctor. You need to be on call twenty-four seven.'

She swallowed. 'Dr McKay wasn't in cellphone range when I ran over him. He can't have been on duty.'

'He was only out of range because Emily has been driving him crazy. She's been driving everyone crazy. Honestly, if I see one more pew ribbon...'

'This wedding's a big deal, huh?'

'Yep.' May put a hand behind the curtain and proffered what was most needed. 'Knickers.'

'Thanks.'

'Bra?'

'Do you normally provide valet service?'

'When I want to talk, I do. Are you sending our Dr McKay away?'

'As soon as I can get to a phone and arrange it, yes.'

'Emily will hate you forever.'

'Hey, it's not my fault.'

'You ran over him.'

'So what am I supposed to do now? Wave a magic wand so he can sail down the aisle tomorrow? The only way he can get married tomorrow is for Emily to follow him to the city and marry him at a bedside ceremony.'

'T-shirt,' May said helpfully. 'Jeans?'

'Great.' Silence while she wiggled into her clothes. Then she pushed the curtain back and emerged.

'Gee,' May said. 'You don't scrub up too badly after all.'

'Thanks.'

'You want to tell them, or shall I?'

'Tell...'

'The happy pair. That the wedding's off. That all those rose petals are going to wilt.'

'Rose petals?'

'Emily's gathered every rose in Birrini,' May said. 'Wheelbarrows of the things.'

Lizzie stared at the woman in front of her, and May stared back.

'Wheelbarrows?'

'Wheelbarrows.'

'Where's Phoebe?' she asked, moving on from this crazy image with some difficulty.

'We're minding her until you've faced Emily,' May told her. 'Phoebe or Emily... We'll take Phoebe any day.'

Dressed and warm and feeling as close to normal as she was going to feel today, Lizzie made her way through to the single ward where Harry lay. As she reached the door she paused. There was the sound of a female voice, strained to breaking point.

'It's not as if you have to walk down the aisle alone. If you have a cast on, you can wait for me on crutches. Then when you reach me you can hold my hand. It'd be better if you didn't use crutches afterwards—for the wedding march—but I'll be able to support you then.'

Lizzie waited, expecting a reply. Nothing.

'Harry, you must. I mean, there are two hundred people invited. We can't tell them it's off.'

Enough. Harry was so drugged he'd agree to anything right now, Lizzie thought, and the sooner she put paid to impossibilities the better. She swung the ward door wide and Emily looked up at her as if she was interrupting something personal. Harry, though, looked across the room to her in real relief.

'Dr Darling.'

'Hi.' She crossed the room to stand beside Emily's chair. He'd regained a little colour. Good. She pushed the cradle back from his leg. The inflatable splint she'd fixed to his leg was holding it rigid. There was still good colour in his toes, she saw with relief. But still...the sooner she had those bones fixed into place by a skilled orthopaedic surgeon the happier she'd be.

'You don't look like a doctor,' he murmured, and she couldn't help but agree.

Her jeans were clean at least, she thought. She tucked her still damp curls behind her ears and tried to look professional. What she needed was a white coat, but every white coat in the place had been bought for Harry. He must be six-two or six-three, she thought, as his coats practically swept the floor on her five-foot-six frame.

And if she didn't look professional... 'Neither do you,' she told him, and he gave her a tired smile.

'I'm not feeling like a doctor. I'm feeling very much like a patient. What's the prognosis?'

She may as well tell it like it was. Now. 'The prognosis is a journey,' she told him. 'To Melbourne. In thirty minutes.'

Emily had been holding Harry's hand. Now she dropped it and turned to Lizzie, her face blanching.

'What do you mean?' she whispered, and Lizzie winced. This wedding was obviously hugely important to Emily—of course it was—but there was no escaping what must be faced. By all of them.

'I mean Harry needs to go to Melbourne tonight,' she said gently, turning back to the man in the bed. 'Harry, I've organised the air ambulance to come straight away. They should be here in about thirty minutes to collect you.'

'Melbourne...' Harry said, bemused.

'You know I can't fix your leg here.'

'Why not?'

So he hadn't fully understood what she'd told him about his leg. 'Would you like to see the

X-rays?' she asked him, producing the films she'd carried in with her. 'That is, if you can stand seeing them without feeling ill?'

He nodded and she held them up to the light. As X-rays went, they were fairly dramatic. This was no hairline fracture. The bones were split and splintered. Even a layman could see the extent of the damage.

There was a long moment's silence as Harry and Emily took them on board together. Then...

'Hell,' Harry said.

That about summed it up, Lizzie thought. She couldn't have put it any better. 'As you say.'

'I've thoroughly busted it.'

'There's a comprehensive medical diagnosis if ever I heard one.' She gave him an appreciative smile. The man had courage. 'It's a complete break of both tibia and fibula. You were lucky it didn't break the skin.'

'More than lucky.' He held out an imperative hand and took the films from her, staring at them intently one after the other. 'I could have blocked the blood supply.'

'You did. I straightened the leg on the road and was really lucky to get circulation again.' She pointed to the film. 'But look at these shards of bone. They're not fixed. I've been lucky—

you've been lucky—but I want that leg operated on as soon as possible.'

He whistled. He stared at the film some more and then whistled again. And then he looked up at her, obviously confused.

'When did you straighten my leg? I can't remember...'

'When you were unconscious.'

'So... I have a headache,' he murmured, thinking it through with obvious care. 'But I'm starting to realise that maybe I owe that bump on my head a lot.'

'It meant I could manipulate your leg while you were unconscious, yes.'

'I guess I should be grateful to you.'

She smiled at that. 'Well, maybe not too grateful. I did run you down.'

'I ran straight into you,' he told her ruefully. 'I thought that road would be deserted. I didn't think anyone would be staying in those holiday units at this time of year. They're awful and the only time they're used is in midsummer.'

'They were the only ones that would let me take my dog.'

He nodded. His eyes were still on the X-rays. He was having trouble focusing, Lizzie thought. The morphine would be doing that. It was a wonder he was awake at all.

'Your leg's hurting?'

'Not much.'

'You make a bad liar,' she said softly. 'I'll give you a top-up before the plane leaves.'

'But…' Emily had been staring at the two of them as if they'd gone mad. 'This is crazy. You've forgotten. Harry can't go on any plane.'

'He must,' Lizzie said gently. 'This leg needs to be fixed. It needs pins to be inserted. Harry needs a skilled orthopaedic surgeon and highly specific equipment. Until Harry has the operation, he can't weight-bear, and the splinters of bone are a real danger to his blood supply. He knows that. Don't you, Harry?'

Harry laid the films down on the coverlet. 'Yes,' he said. And sighed. 'I do.' He sighed again.

Something wasn't right.

Lizzie stared down at him. He stared straight back and her initial impression intensified. Was it possible? She must be imagining it, she told herself, but for just a moment she thought she'd detected a note of real relief in his voice. And…the faintest trace of laughter?

She must have been imagining it. There was no such relief in Emily's tone—or in her expression. The woman faced Lizzie with desperation, and her face was more shocked than Harry's.

'If he can't weight-bear... That just means traction. You can do it here and he'll just have to use a wheelchair. We can do that.'

But Lizzie was shaking her head. 'Traction can't guarantee Harry the same results as pinning,' she told her. 'You don't want Harry to end up with one leg longer than the other.' Then, as Emily's face said she wasn't so sure, Lizzie pressed on.

'Emily, look again at that film,' she said gently. 'When Harry was first injured the blood supply was completely blocked. I was lucky enough to get the leg into a position where the blood vessels are operating but I don't know how permanent that is. The X-rays are telling me there are loose splinters of bone that could block the blood supply again. He has to be operated on and that need is urgent. I don't have an anaesthetist and I don't have the equipment, even if I was trained to do this sort of operation. Which I'm not. I'm sorry, Emily, but there is no choice.'

'There must be.'

'There isn't.'

'Harry, make her see...' There were tears rolling down the woman's face. Good grief,

Lizzie thought. She was verging on the hysterical.

It was only a wedding.

She opened her mouth to say something, but Harry was there before her. His hand came out and caught his fiancée's, gripping it tight. 'No, Em. It's you who has to see. Dr Darling's right. I need to go to Melbourne. We need to postpone the wedding.'

'If you give us a list of guests, May and I will sit down tonight and contact them,' Lizzie told them. 'May's already offered. She tells me the hospital is quiet. Only five patients.'

'I'll need to go through patient lists before I go,' Harry said sharply, and Lizzie thought, Gee, he sounds more worried about his patients than he does about his wedding.

Maybe he was. Weddings weren't her cup of tea either.

'May's shown me the ward sheets. There's nothing I can't deal with.'

'Unless Phoebe goes into labour,' Harry told her, and Lizzie found herself smiling at the man. He was grinning up at her—a faint half-grin, but magnetic for all that.

He did have the most wonderful smile...

'I already checked to see if there was a vet in town before I took this job,' she told him, fascinated, and even more fascinated as his eyes crinkled into laughter.

'You mean you checked the vet situation but you didn't check the medical scene?'

'I checked what was important. Though if I'd known the town had only one suicidal doctor...' She gasped and caught herself. What was she doing, giving him cheek? Laughing with him? She should be checking his sedation and wishing him a safe journey.

She should be moving right on.

'Is there anything you need before I go?' she asked stiffly, and his smile died. Beside him, Emily was standing ashen with shock, and he gave her a worried look.

'Something for Em?'

'A sedative?'

'She's been looking forward to this wedding for a long time.'

She's been looking forward to this wedding? Nothing about him, she noticed.

But that could wait. It wasn't her business.

'Will you go with Harry?' she asked, and the other woman turned to her with blind eyes.

'Of course I'll go with Harry. And I don't need anything. I don't need a sedative.' But her voice was wobbling dangerously.

'Can I ring your parents? Someone to help you?'

'Every single one of Em's relatives has been in town for over a week,' Harry said ruefully. 'But they'll be no support at all.' His grip on Emily's hand tightened and his voice became urgent. 'Em, you need to stay here. Lizzie's going to need help.'

'I'm coming with you. Dr Darling can cope by herself. She got us into this mess. My mother can cope with wedding things. She can set another date…'

'Leave setting the date for a while,' Lizzie told her. She put a hand on Emily's shoulder and looked sideways at Harry. She didn't understand what was going on here. There were very interesting undertones… 'Let me call your mother now,' she offered. 'I'll give you something to help settle you for the trip. You've had a shock as well as Harry and you need to be kind to yourself. But meanwhile you need to pack, for yourself and for Harry. The plane will be here very soon.'

Emily cast her a look that was more than desperate. 'I don't need any sedative,' she snapped. 'Of course I don't. Don't be stupid. I'll pack. I'll talk to my mother.' She shook her head as if casting off a nightmare. 'I'll do it now.'

She cast one despairing glance at Harry. 'If you're sure...'

'We're sure, Em,' Harry said gently, and Em gave a last angry gasp.

'Fine, then. I'll pack.'

And she left Lizzie and Harry alone.

'I'm sorry.' With Em gone, Lizzie lifted the chart at the end of the bed and started writing. There'd be a doctor on the air ambulance, and the medical team in Melbourne would need to know what she'd done.

'Don't be sorry.' Harry looked remarkably cheerful for someone who was in pain, who'd almost lost his leg and who'd just missed out on his wedding. 'It was more Em's wedding than mine anyway.'

'You only need to put it back a week or so. If the leg can be pinned you'll be weight-bearing in no time.'

'I'm not getting married until I can put my dinner suit on. That'll be weeks.'

'May says the ambulance service will bring you back as soon as the orthopods let you go.' She'd perched on the seat Em had vacated and she wrote up the drug sheet. 'That should be no more than a few days.'

'You'll stay on?'

'I shouldn't,' she said bitterly, setting down her pen and gazing at him with resignation. 'I've been tricked into coming here.'

'Not by me. And you hit me.'

'You ran into my car.'

'I did,' he conceded. 'Running in the middle of the road isn't exactly a sensible thing to do.'

'Your mind was on other things?'

'I'd had a bit much wedding.' He winced and she rose to adjust the cradle over his leg.

'I'll give you more morphine just before you're moved.'

'I'd appreciate it. Lizzie…the patients…'

'You have Mrs Kelly in One with a brand-new daughter who's just been transferred back after delivering in Melbourne. You have Ted Parker in Two with angina. Robby Bradly and Pete Scoresby aged ten and eleven respectively are in Three with multiple abrasions and a couple of greenstick fractures after their cubby house decided to fall twenty feet from a eucalypt. They should be right to go home tomorrow as soon as their respective mothers have recovered from the shock. And Lillian Mark is in Four with anorexia.'

'May's told you everything.'

'I've even read the patient notes,' she told him, and if her voice sounded a wee bit smug, who could blame her? She'd been so out of control it was nice to be able to gather a little bit of normality. Like reading patient notes.

But Harry was frowning. Concentrating. 'It's Lillian I wanted to talk to you about,' he managed. 'She should be in a psychiatric ward but her parents won't hear of it. I'm worried about her. There's the potential for suicide.'

'She won't suicide on my patch.'

'You're very sure.'

'I've dealt with anorexic kids before.' She softened. 'Don't worry. I'll talk to her now and I'll run ward rounds four times a day.'

'You can't stay out at that damned holiday unit.'

'No.' She shook her head. 'I can't. Phoebe's going to kill herself if I try.'

'And you can't be on call out there. You're the only doctor. You need to be able to be contacted.'

She thought about that and didn't like it. Twenty-four seven on call wasn't what she'd intended. 'You were running out of cellphone range,' she told him.

'For half an hour. Because every phone call was about the wedding.'

She wrinkled her nose. 'Heavy, huh?'

'You have no idea.'

'So maybe I saved you from a fate worse than death?'

'Or maybe I'll just have to go through the whole damned palaver again.'

'You're a big boy. You can cope.' She rose and tilted her head on one side, taking him in. 'I need to go. May's trying to find me accommodation where Phoebe's welcome.' She sighed. 'I'm not holding my breath.'

'Use the doctor's quarters.'

'What—your place?'

'I won't be there.'

'You'll be back in three or four days.'

'There's two bedrooms and most of my stuff is at Emily—at our new home.'

She thought about it. Of course. They were marrying. He'd be well out of the doctor's quarters.

'You reckon the hospital board will object to Phoebe?'

'Probably, but tell them it's a package deal. You and Phoebe or nothing. I think you'll find they have no choice.' He closed his eyes and winced again. 'Hell, when am I due for more morph?'

She checked her watch. 'I'll give you some now. You sound like you're getting addicted.'

'You have no idea.'

She smiled and rang the bell. Ten seconds later May's bright face appeared around the door. 'Problem?'

'We need a nice healthy dose of morphine so the good doctor can sleep all the way to Melbourne,' Lizzie told her, and May nodded.

'Coming right up.' She hesitated. 'Though you might want to add a bit for Emily. I think she intends to weep all the way there.'

'Make her stay,' Harry said weakly, and May's eyes creased in sympathy.

'No can do,' she said softly. 'Your fiancée. Your problem. And maybe our Dr Darling has given you breathing space to figure it out.'

CHAPTER THREE

Memo:
I will not brain Emily.
I will understand why Emily is as she is.
I will not worry about what long-term dam-age has been done to this leg. Dr Darling's organised the best orthopaedic surgeons in Melbourne. The pain will ease when they've pinned it. I'll be weight-bearing in no time. I'll be fine.
I will not talk weddings.
I will not think of how cute Dr Lizzie Darling is when she's worried…
I will not brain Emily.

HARRY McKAY was scheduled to return to Birrini by road ambulance six days after he left. Emily was not to accompany him.

'She'd organised to take the next three weeks off for her honeymoon,' May told Lizzie. 'So now her mother's decided to take her shopping. She's figured she can spend the next few weeks shopping for fittings for their new home.'

'Um…' They were standing in the nurses' station. Harry's ambulance was due any minute and Lizzie was aware of a pinch of nerves. She'd done a decent job holding this little community together, but it was going to be harder having Harry looking over her shoulder. 'Is Emily usually…?'

'Neurotic?' May grinned and shook her head. 'Nope. Well, maybe. You tell me. She's been the charge nurse here for the last five years. She's quiet and competent and sensible. The perfect nurse really. Then our Dr Harry decides she'd be the perfect wife and she loses it completely. I mean…I've never seen so much fuss about a wedding in my life.'

'Harry doesn't like it?'

'I think he wonders what he's got himself into,' May said bluntly. 'I have a feeling he chose Emily because she was sensible and now…'

'He chose her because she was sensible?'

'Yeah, I know.' May grinned. 'Daft, the pair of them. Not like my Tom who chose me because he couldn't keep his hands or his eyes or his dirty mind off me.' Her grin deepened. 'Me and Tom…we're not exactly sensible but, gee, I love it.'

'I imagine you do.' Here was yet another gem of local knowledge. Lizzie was feeling more and more stunned every day she stayed here. In the last week she'd learned more about the individuals who made up the community of Birrini than she knew about anyone in her huge teaching hospital in Queensland. There was no way you finished here at five o'clock and walked out, closing the door behind you. Your patients would greet you in the grocery store or they'd drop in an apple pie they'd just baked or a fish they'd just caught or they'd appear with a bone for the poor wee doggie...

The poor wee doggie was growing huger by the minute. The Birrini population had discovered that Phoebe was the reason Lizzie had come here, so it was a communal responsibility to see her content.

'I reckon she's having quads,' Lizzie muttered, and May looked at her, startled.

'Who, Emily?'

'Phoebe.'

'Your mind's not running on the one track, then, is it?'

'No.'

'Neither is mine,' May admitted, giving her a sideways glance that was more than a little calculating. 'It's running in all sorts of directions.' She grinned and picked up a bundle of linen behind her. 'Well, I'll be off to make up a bed for his lordship. But you know the way my mind's suddenly heading?'

'What?'

'Two weeks without Emily.' May's grin broadened. 'Two weeks without Emily and our Dr McKay is stuck with you and Phoebe and the quads. Very interesting is all I can say. Very interesting indeed.'

Which was nonsense. Lizzie was left staring after her. She wasn't making sense.

Nothing was making sense.

'I'll go and visit Lillian,' she told herself. Lillian, the anorexic kid in Room Four, was practically the only one of her patients who wasn't self-treating. She dug her hands deep into the pockets of the white coat which May had kindly taken up for her and thought, At least with Lillian I feel like a doctor.

She was here for medicine. Harry McKay was a patient.

So there was no reason at all that she should all of a sudden be suffering from goose-bumps.

He was fine. He was terrific.

The ambulance boys wheeled Harry's chair into the hospital entrance and Lizzie had to pinch herself to believe it was the same man. His leg was stuck out on a support in front, but he was shrugging off his helpers and propelling himself forward, looking about him like a man who'd been away from home for months.

Lizzie didn't move. Not yet. She stood where she was behind the desk in the nurses' station, taking in the sight of him before he saw her.

He was wearing jeans cut off at the knees. A sweatshirt. Trainers. Not the ones she'd hauled off in the mud but ones that were considerably cleaner.

He wasn't wearing a cast but a back-slab with bandages to keep it in place. He must be securely plated and pinned, then. But...not enough to be on crutches yet?

What else? She should be behaving like a doctor, concentrating on things like his leg and the fact that he looked healthy. But she was distracted.

She'd never seen his hair completely dry, she thought inconsequentially. Deeply black, it looked soft and thick and curly and...nice?

The whole package looked nice, she decided. He was laughing up at something one of the paramedics had said and his whole face was lit with his laughter. There was something about this man that had the capacity to light the darkness...

Now she was being stupid. Teenage crush stupid. She gave herself a mental slap to the right ear and stepped forward.

'Welcome home, Dr McKay.'

His laughter faded. His wheelchair stopped dead and he stared up at her.

'Lizzie,' he said softly. 'Lizzie. So I didn't imagine...'

His voice trailed off and she frowned. He hadn't imagined what?

Professional. She needed to be professional. Doctor receiving a patient transferring from paramedics.

Right. Another mental slap.

'Do you have Dr McKay's notes?' she asked the senior of the two ambulance officers, and the uniformed paramedic shook his head.

'I have the notes,' Harry said. 'They're in my bag. I'll show them to you later if you need to see them.'

'Of course I need to see them. You're my patient.'

'I'm not a patient.'

The paramedic rolled his eyes at her and winked. 'You'll have your hands full with this one, I reckon. Straitjackets and enemas and bedpans, I reckon.'

'Hmm.' She smiled. 'I can manage that. Meanwhile, can you take Dr McKay into Room Five?'

'I'm not going into a ward,' Harry snapped. 'I'm going home.'

'But…' Lizzie blinked. 'You can't.'

'Why not?'

There was only one answer to that. 'Because I'm in your home.'

His eyes narrowed, creasing again into the beginnings of a smile. 'So you're in my home. You're not in my bed, I hope?'

'Well, no…'

'Then what's the problem? There are two bedrooms.'

'All your gear's been moved out. May said it was over at the house you share with Emily.'

'I don't share a house with Emily.'

'I mean…well, after you're married…' She was tripping over her tongue here and the two paramedics were looking on with increasing interest.

'After I'm married then maybe I'll move out of my house. Not before.'

'None of your personal things are there.'

'Only because Emily's brothers moved them the day before the wedding. Before I could stop them. I'll send Jim over to bring back what I need.'

Lizzie shook her head. She was really confused.

She needed to focus.

'I share your house with Phoebe,' she said, desperately trying to think through reasons why he couldn't share a house with her. Reasons that were logical and not the reasons that were filling her head with panic. 'Phoebe would have to be the worst type of dog for a man in a wheelchair.'

'I'm only in a wheelchair on sufferance to stop these people getting sued if I fall flat on my face. I'm weight-bearing.'

'With sticks.'

'With sticks,' he conceded.

'Phoebe eats sticks.'

'They're aluminium.'

'I don't think she's smart enough to know the difference.'

Silence. 'Don't you want me to live with you?' he asked, his voice suddenly dangerous, and she blinked.

'Um… No?'

'Why? Am I so dangerous?'

Dangerous, she thought wildly. Yes. The description was apt. That twinkle was definitely dangerous.

'I'm not a threat,' he continued, and she knew he definitely was.

But she wasn't telling him so. 'I didn't say you were,' she said with asperity. 'Phoebe's nearly killed you once. I'm worried that the next time she might finish you off completely.'

'So you've warned me. You've done your best. Now let me go home.'

'You need to stay in hospital.'

'No. I need to stay with you.'

They had quite an audience now. May had come out of the ward behind Lizzie and was watching in appreciative silence. The ambulance officers were, frankly, enjoying themselves. Even Lillian, the wraith-like teenager who lay in her bed each day and said nothing to anyone, was peering around her door in interest.

'Go on, love,' the older of the ambulance officers said. 'Let him live with you.' He grinned at the pair of them. 'I dare say he's housetrained by now.'

'And you did say you weren't sleeping in his bed,' the other one added. 'That's got to make it all right.'

'It'd be better fun if she was,' May offered, and Lizzie winced.

'Will you lot just butt out?'

'Why should they?' For heaven's sake, Harry looked as if he was enjoying himself. He caught sight of Lillian peeping around the door and he smiled. 'What you reckon, Lill? Do you think Dr Darling should let me live with her?'

They all looked up. Lillian. The girl was almost pathologically shy. Lizzie had spent the last six days working to gain her confidence, but there was a long way to go. She'd retreat, Lizzie thought. She'd blush and stammer and disappear.

But amazingly Lillian held her ground.

'I don't think you should refuse to share a house with Dr McKay,' she told Lizzie in a voice that was so near the tone that Lizzie had used with her that morning that she blinked in astonishment. 'You might destroy his self-confidence if you do. Self-confidence is a very fragile thing. It's more important even than legs.'

There. Lillian blushed to the roots of her hair but she didn't retreat. She met Lizzie's eyes and there was a hint of defiance—even a hint of laughter—in the girl's face. Amazing.

And after that impressive little lecture there was nowhere for Lizzie to go at all.

So what was a girl to do? She threw her hands in the air and she surrendered.

'Fine,' she told them. 'Don't stay in the hospital, then. See if I care. I dare say those notes under your arm say bed-rest and bedpans for six weeks.'

'They do not.'

'Are you intending to let me see them?'

He grinned. 'Nope.'

'Well, then…'

'Well, then, let's move on.' Harry looked up to the ambulance officers and he smiled. 'We'll let you boys go. As you can see, Dr Darling is in charge of my future treatment.' Then he turned back to Lizzie.

'OK, Dr Darling,' he told her. 'I'm ready. Would you like to take me home?'

'What's this?'

Harry pushed himself through the swing doors separating hospital from doctor's quarters and stopped dead.

When Lizzie had walked into this place a week ago she'd found it had been spartan to the point of coldness. The place had been designed for functionality rather than beauty.

It wasn't any more, though. Lizzie looked down at the man in the wheelchair, noted his look of incredulity and thought, Whoops. There was only one thing to do here. Move straight to the offensive.

'It was horrible,' she told him.

'Pardon?'

'Your decor. It was horrible.'

He stared some more and appeared to consider what she'd said. 'You know, if you invited me to stay in your home I wouldn't have thought the first thing I'd say to you about it was that the decor was horrible,' he remarked thoughtfully.

'You might if it was awful.'

'I mightn't if it was rude. As it is. As you are.'

'Don't tell me you liked it?'

'It mightn't have been much,' he said, his tone wounded, 'but it was home.'

She cast him a suspicious look. She didn't know him well enough yet to know whether he was joking. He stared at her, deadpan, and she still didn't know.

'Oh, come on. It's not your decor. It's some hospital administrator's idea of decor. This is much better.' She paused, suddenly doubtful. Maybe some people liked beige walls. 'Isn't it?'

And thankfully he decided to concede. 'It is,' he said slowly, wheeling himself forward so he can see. 'It's…amazing.'

It was. Relieved, Lizzie gazed about her, smugly satisfied by what she'd achieved in six short days.

'How on earth did you get this done?'

'Miss Morrison came in to get her flu shot,' she said.

He stared. 'Pardon?'

'Miss Morrison, Birrini's third-grade teacher.'

'I know who Susan Morrison is.'

'Then you'll know she has lists.'

'I know.' Harry uttered a groan, obviously remembering. Susan Morrison's lists were the bane of any doctor's life. She believed in getting her money's worth at each consultation. She'd save up complaints until she had a list full of her problems—and sometimes those of her students for good measure—and then book in for a short consultation and expect the doctor to solve everything in one hit. 'I'm sorry.'

'Don't be,' Lizzie told him, feeling immeasurably better now that the accusation had gone out of his tone. 'I like Sue Morrison. Old school, but nice. Anyway, she was having a whinge so I thought I'd whinge right back.'

Lizzie was feeling really strange here and the easiest thing to do was concentrate on patients. Neutral ground. Medicine. After all, that was the only thing she had in common with this man. Wasn't it?

'You whinged right back?' He sounded bemused.

'I told her how cold it was in Birrini and how much I was missing Queensland and how awful this apartment is. How…beige.'

'I like beige.'

'Really?' She gave a dramatic shudder. 'Beige is awful.'

'Awful?'

'There wasn't one single picture on the wall,' she said accusingly, and he looked around him in increasing wonder.

'There is now.'

'Well, of course. Miss Morrison decided right there and then that she'd fix things for me. So she marched back to her third-graders and announced the Great Queensland Painting Competition. She had each of them draw their impression of Northern Queensland.' Lizzie paused for breath as she gazed around the apartment. It looked great, she thought as she surveyed the once beige walls plastered with posters. 'What do you think?' she asked. 'Aren't they wonderful?'

He had to agree, she thought. How could he not? The pictures were as varied as the kids who'd drawn them. There were huge yellow suns, palm trees, stick-figure surfers sweeping shorewards on crests of blue, blue waves. There were crocodiles and octopuses and crowds on beaches and fun fairs and yachts and...

And summer.

'It warms me up just to look at them,' she told him, deeply satisfied. 'And, as well as that, it's fixed another thing on Miss Morrison's list.'

'Yeah?'

He was starting to sound off balance, Lizzie thought. Good. He had her off balance just looking at her. It was about time the tables were turned. 'Yeah,' she agreed. 'Amy Dunstan is eight years old and she's being bullied.'

Harry frowned at that. 'I know Amy,' he told her. 'Her family's had a really tough time.'

'I gathered that. Miss Morrison told me. It must be so dreadful to lose a child to meningitis.'

'It happened two years ago.' Harry had parked his chair under the table and was still staring at the posters. But he was obviously thinking of the Dunstans. 'Scott died just before the family moved here. They came here to try and break with the past. Break with shadows.'

'It hasn't worked,' Lizzie said bluntly. 'Scott was a year older than Amy and that house is set up as a shrine to him. Still. Two years on.'

'You've been there?'

'Of course I've been there. Amy's problems were on Miss Morrison's list. I had to do something.'

'She asked you to do a house call?'

'No, but I just happened to be walking Phoebe past the Dunstans' and she needed a drink of water.'

'You just happened...Where is Phoebe?' he asked, fascinated, but she shook her head.

'Don't you want to know about Amy?'

'Yes. Yes, of course I want to know about Amy.'

'Well.' Lizzie beamed. She was deeply satisfied at the way things were working out here and she couldn't quite keep the smugness from her face. 'We—Amy's mother and I—talked about Amy's lack of self-esteem and the way it seems to be the cause of the bullying. Kids are cruel and they'll always pick on someone who's down already. That's what Miss Morrison thinks and as Miss Morrison's been teaching for thirty years I dare say she's right.'

'I dare say.'

She cast him a suspicious look. His tone was too bland. But she decided to overlook it. This once.

'Well, she is. I'm sure. Oh, Harry, the Dunstan house is appalling. You walk in and there's this huge picture of Scott right in the entrance hall. There are pictures of him right through the house with candles that seem to be lit all the time. It's awful. Like a funeral parlour, only worse. Mrs Dunstan can't talk about him without crying.'

'I'm sorry but I don't see...'

'There's not a single picture of Amy,' she told him, and her tone was accusing.

Which was hardly fair.

'Isn't there?' Harry's smile had faded completely now. 'I haven't seen it—the family has never invited me in—but I can imagine. I know the family is in distress but what to do about it...'

'I did something about it.'

'You did?'

'I told her she had two children,' Lizzie said bluntly. 'I said if she didn't want to lose Amy as well as Scott then she needed to think about her daughter for a bit as well as her son.'

'Just like that.'

'It sounds easy.' Lizzie hesitated, then shrugged and crossed to the kitchenette to fill the kettle. 'You want some coffee?'

'Please.'

It was easier with her back to him. She didn't feel so self-conscious. So aware that he might be judging her.

'I showed Mary Dunstan the figures of adolescent depression linked to suicide,' she told him, and was aware of a deep silence behind her.

'You told her…'

'Someone had to.' Lizzie turned and faced him. 'I told her any eight-year-old living in that house would figure the only way to get love and attention was to be dead. I asked Mary if that's what she and her husband intended Amy to believe.'

'My God, Lizzie…'

'I was horrible,' Lizzie said with a faintly embarrassed laugh. 'But someone had to be. Anyway, I talked for ages and Mary had a bit of a cry but I told her that wasn't any use either and then I offered them a puppy.'

'A puppy.' He sounded stunned. 'Not...one of Phoebe's?'

'Of course one of Phoebe's.' She was more sure of herself now. Going to the home of one of Harry's patients and putting her oar in where she wasn't sure she was welcome had seemed a bit...intrusive? But surely he couldn't object to this.

'Actually, I didn't give the puppy to Amy straight away,' she admitted. 'I told her mother she was going to win it in my drawing competition. If she agreed. By the way, that's Amy's picture up there.' She pointed over the sink to a vast painting of a kid on a surfboard. 'Isn't it good?'

'They're all good.'

She beamed. 'They are, aren't they? They're all fantastic. So I asked Lillian if she'd do it and Lillian agreed with me straight away.'

'Whoa.' Harry looked like a man right out of his depth. He put up his hand to stop her. 'Lillian?' The anorexic teenager he'd just seen giving him cheek? 'What's Lillian got to do with this?'

'Lillian is acting as our judge. Did you know, she got first prize for art last year and she won a state-wide competition? The Avis Baxter wa-

tercolour competition. I'm told it's really pres-
tigious. May tells me her parents wouldn't even
let her go to Melbourne to collect the award—
they belittle her talent—but she's really good.'

He nodded, bemused. 'Yes,' he said slowly.
'I did know that. Her parents disapprove—
which I have a huge feeling is one of the reasons
she's anorexic—but she's very good.'

'Well.' She regarded him with satisfaction.
'There you go, then. I brought Lillian in some
paints the other day and she's redecorating the
walls in the kids' ward. Which is keeping her
mind off her neurosis nicely. But meanwhile I
had a talk to Lillian about Amy's depression and
she says she feels just like that sometimes, only
blacker. She's so sympathetic. The art prize was
a big thing for her, she reckons, so we've rigged
this…'

'You've rigged this?'

'Did you know you sound very like a record-
ing?' she said kindly. 'Or a parrot. No. Don't
apologise. You've been sick. You're forgiven.'
She paused, giving him space to answer back—
but he looked too stunned to even try.

'Anyway we decided a little rigging was in
order,' she continued. 'I have Amy's mum's
permission for her to win a puppy. So…first
prize for the competition is first pick of
Phoebe's puppies. It wouldn't work if I hadn't

rigged it. I don't believe in kids winning pets. They have to really want them. But tomorrow there's going to be a full school assembly. Every kid in the school wants one of Phoebe's puppies—Miss Morrison and I really hyped them up. Phoebe's even been into the school to be introduced. The build-up's huge and, thanks to Lillian's conspiracy, Amy's going to win. She's going to be the envy of every child in the school. The kids will have to be nice to her if they want to play with the puppy. Miss Morrison says it's the very best thing she could think of. Oh, and Mrs Dunstan's taken down the shrine and put up a picture of Scott and Amy together. So…what do you think?'

She paused for breath.

What did he think?

She'd been gabbling, she decided. She'd been interfering in things that weren't her business, but for the last few days she hadn't cared. She was stuck here in this little community. She was here to do the job as locum and she'd walk away in a few weeks and probably never come near Birrini again. Meanwhile the tiny township was being incredibly nice to her and her grandma's crazy dog, so it wouldn't hurt to get involved. For a while.

At least, that's what she'd been telling her-self, but now, looking at Harry's stunned face, she wasn't so sure.

'Do you disapprove?' she asked.

'Why would I disapprove?'

'You like a beige apartment, remember?'

'When did I say I like a beige apartment?'

'Ten minutes ago.'

'I must have been mad.'

She met his eyes. He was telling the truth, she thought, and cheered up immeasurably. For some strange reason what this man thought of her was becoming of paramount importance. Not that she intended to let him see that. So, act…insouciant? Was that the word?

Probably.

'That's what I thought,' she said cheerfully. 'Coffee?' She held out a mug and he took it without appearing to notice. He was still staring at her and his gaze was starting to unnerve her.

Move on…

'Now,' she said, a lot more briskly and effi-ciently than she felt, 'I need to do a clinic before dinner. I have three house calls to make and Phoebe to collect so I need to go. Can I give you a hand getting into bed before I leave?'

'You're not helping me get into bed,' he told her, startled.

'No?'

He thought about it. 'No. And there's no need to sound wistful. No!'

Lizzie grinned. 'Believe it or not, I wasn't sounding wistful.'

'Really?' The laughter in his eyes was wicked.

'Absolutely really,' she told him with all the asperity she could muster. She needed to get this on a formal footing right now. 'So there's no need to sound hopeful. You're practically a married man. With a broken leg. You're no use at all to a single girl like me.'

'I suppose I'm not,' he said, doleful all of a sudden, and she had to chuckle.

'Good. As long as we have that clear. So how do you intend to get into bed without me...I mean, without help?'

Harry was laughing at her. The rat! The logistics of sharing an apartment with this man were growing more complex by the minute.

'If I wanted to go to bed—which I don't—then I'd put my pyjamas on,' he told her blandly, and she blinked.

'Over your back-slab?'

'Over my back-slab. I've cut a slit in the pyjama leg.'

'Oh, very practical.'

He laughed, but he obviously didn't intend her to have the last word. 'Quiet, woman,' he ordered. 'Hear me out. There's no need to focus on my pyjama slit quite yet—because I don't intend to get into bed. I'm only in this damned chair until someone provides me with sticks. The guys left my crutches back in Melbourne.'

She fixed him with a look that said she didn't believe a word. 'Are you kidding me?'

'I'm not kidding you.'

'You left your crutches in Melbourne. That's something I really believe. Like Miss Morrison being told by her third-graders that the dog ate their homework.'

He stared up at her, wounded to the core. 'Don't you believe me?'

'Nope. There's no way you'd be permitted to be weight-bearing yet.'

'I can use crutches without weight-bearing. I broke my ankle when I was seven. I'm a champion at hopping.'

'Hopping. Six days post-surgery.'

'That's the one.' He beamed and she refused to be disconcerted by a beam. No matter how distracting this particular beam was.

'Let me see your patient notes.'

'No!'

'I'll ring up the orthopod. Let's ask him if you're supposed to be hopping.'

'I'm fine.'

'You can't hop if you don't have crutches.'

Stalemate. She eyed him thoughtfully. He eyed her back.

'Oh, for heaven's sake. The leg's really secure. The pin and plate are holding everything in place and if it wasn't for the wound itself and the swelling I'd have a nice light fibreglass cast that would stop you worrying completely.'

'So it's OK for me to worry now?'

He sighed. 'You're like a terrier with a bone.'

'A broken bone,' she agreed. 'Or two bones. Tib and fib. Let me read your notes.'

They glared at each other. And kept on glaring. And he capitulated first.

'Read them, then,' he said, goaded, and thrust the notes at her.

She grinned. 'There's a good little patient.'

'Lizzie…'

'Mmm?'

'I'm your boss, remember?'

'And you're my patient.'

'Just go and do your clinic—my clinic. Read my notes in your own time, but in the meantime leave me be. I'll wheel myself over to the storeroom and find some crutches.'

'I'll wheel you. May can bring you back. After I've read the notes.' She plonked herself down at the kitchen table. 'Talk amongst yourself,' she told him. 'I'm reading.'

'Lizzie…'

'Yes?'

'I don't think I can live with you.'

She didn't bother to look up at that. She couldn't. He'd make her laugh and his laugh was altogether too dangerous. 'Hey, are we back where we started? That's what I was saying. And you haven't even met Phoebe yet.' She went back to reading.

'So...' He drank his coffee and stared at her bent head, baffled. 'Where's Phoebe?'

She still didn't look up, forcing herself to focus on the orthopod's close-written notes. 'Being Phoebe-sat,' she told him. 'If I leave her here alone she destroys the door. Jim's had to replace it once already. We had to use four posters to cover the damage. So now the locals have organised a roster.' She smiled up at him briefly before burying her nose once again. '"Weight-bearing in small bursts after the cast with plaster boot fitted",' she read. '"No weight-bearing until the cast is fitted".'

'Thus the hopping...'

She ignored him. 'Physiotherapy. This town doesn't have a physio.'

'I don't need a physio.'

'Yes, you do. Just lucky you have me.' She buried her nose again.

'What do you mean—just lucky I have you?' he asked, and she wiggled herself further into her chair and smiled.

'I did three years of physiotherapy before I started medicine.'

'How old are you?' Harry looked shaken.

'Twenty-nine.'

'You sound about ten.'

'Gee, thanks.'

'Why did you start physio?'

'I thought it would be good. It was good. Only halfway through I decided I wanted to do everything.' She frowned, lifting an X-ray and holding it up to the light. 'Heck, you were lucky, Harry. Do you realise how close you came to losing the whole leg?'

'I know,' he said shortly, and she finally looked at him across the table. Really looked at him.

'You know you'll be fine. The pins work really well and Max Carter's the best orthopod. He's talking about a hundred per cent recovery.'

'I know.'

'So?'

'So I'm frustrated. And I don't intend to use you for physio.'

'Well.' She laid the notes on the table. 'It doesn't hurt to see a man frustrated. There should be more of it, I reckon. And if you don't agree to use me for physio then I'll simply remove every crutch in the storeroom right now. What's it to be, Dr McKay?'

'I don't have to—'

'You do have to. You're being childish.'

'Me...childish?'

'Most men are. I guess you can't help it. Now, do you agree to treatment so I can organise these crutches, or am I going to ring May and tell her to move the crutches fast?'

'You'd really...?'

'I'd really.'

He stared up at her. Goaded. Something was working behind his eyes, she thought, but she couldn't figure it out. He seemed totally bemused. But there was only one option he could take, and that was the sensible one. Finally he sighed and spread his hands.

'Fine.'

'There's a good boy,' she told him, and grinned. She came behind his chair and pushed him toward the door. 'Obedience. That's what I want. Now, let the nice doctor take you for a walk in your pushchair before she gets back to her work.'

'Lizzie?'

'Yes?'

'Do you want your ears boxed?'

'Kinky,' she said. 'Very kinky. Of course I don't want my ears boxed. You must be missing your Emily.'

Harry was reduced to stunned silence.

CHAPTER FOUR

Memo:
Real doctors do not whimper and disinte-
grate into their wimpy wheelchairs.
Real doctors stand up for more than five
minutes.
I will not fall flat on my face.
I will smile at Mrs Jordon and try not to
think that a ninety-three-year-old heart pa-
tient is travelling with more speed than I am.
I will not think of Lizzie.
I will not interfere… I will not try and
reach the end of the corridor where I can
hear her voice.
Damn, I can't reach the end of the corri-
dor. Not on crutches.
I will just sit back in my wheelchair for a
moment and maybe let it roll forward. Just to
stay out of the way while I have a rest. Not
because I can hear every word she and
Lillian are saying…

'So how's it working out?'

'What?' Lizzie was sitting on Lillian's bed,

95

watching the girl eat her dinner. Or rather watching the girl trying not to eat her dinner.

This was a huge, long-running battle. There were lots of psychological things happening here. By rights Lillian should be in a purpose-designed psychiatric unit, getting the treatment she needed, but that was out of the question.

'My daughter's not a nutter,' Richard Mark had growled when Lizzie had raised the issue. 'She shouldn't even be in hospital, much less a mental institution.'

'It's not a mental institution. It's just a centre for kids with problems like Lillian. Lillian's about forty per cent below minimum recommended body weight. She's dangerously ill.'

'Her mother can feed her.'

'You know that's why Dr McKay put her in hospital,' Lizzie had told him. 'Lillian's been eating when forced, but then making herself vomit afterwards. If she loses any more weight she'll go into kidney failure. She'll die.'

The shock tactics had worked a little—but not enough.

'OK. She can stay with you. But not a mental institution. No way.'

At least the hospital was quiet, Lizzie thought thankfully. Someone needed to stay with Lillian while she ate, supervising every mouthful that went in, and then she had to be watched for at least an hour afterwards or the meal came straight back up.

In the emergency medicine Lizzie was accustomed to, she'd never helped with such a patient, but the first night she'd been here all the staff had been busy and she'd volunteered. To her astonishment she'd found it incredibly rewarding. She was gaining real rapport with the troubled teenager and there was a distinct flush to the girl's cheeks which hadn't been there a week ago.

If she was weighed Lizzie was sure she'd have gained a little, she thought, looking at her now as she toyed with her meal, but there was no way she was letting the girl near scales. She had to agree she was looking better before she could horrify herself with the concept of gaining weight.

'You and Dr Harry.' The girl lifted a fork loaded with a whole pea and looked at it dubiously.

'Three peas,' Lizzie told her. She leaned over, took the fork from the girl's fingers, reloaded the peas and offered it to her again. 'Eat.'

'But—'

'Down.'

Lillian hesitated. And swallowed.

'Great,' Lizzie asked. 'We'll have you as cuddly as me in no time. Lillian, do you think I'm fat?' She took the fork and reloaded it.

'You?'

'Me.'

Lillian looked at her, assessing. 'Those jeans look cute,' she said.

'They do, don't they?' Lizzie wiggled herself on the bedclothes and looked across at the mirror. 'And I know this T-shirt is tight but if I lose any more weight then my boobs shrink. There's nothing worse than shrunk boobs.'

'Isn't there?'

'No,' Lizzie said definitely. 'Eat.'

Lillian looked at her fork. She looked at Lizzie's…boobs? And ate.

'Terrific,' Lizzie told her, and poked out her chest. 'You'll have nice boobs in no time.'

'You don't think my boobs are nice now?' Lillian asked anxiously, and Lizzie shook her head.

'They're pimples, not boobs. Real women are cuddly. Like me.'

'Does Dr McKay think you're cuddly?'

'I bet he does.'

'And you're sharing a house with him.'

'Eat that sausage,' Lizzie growled. 'All up.'

'Why? I don't need it.'

'You do need it. We're in boob-growing mode here. Besides, if you want to talk about grown-up stuff you have to act like a grown-up.'

'Like...' Lillian nibbled an end of the sausage. 'Like what?'

'Well, are we talking about what a hunk Dr McKay is?'

'Mmm.' Lillian smiled. Girl talk. She was very definitely interested. 'You think he's a hunk?'

'Bite and swallow and I'll tell you.'

'OK.'

'Once more.'

'That's cheating.'

'I won't tell you.'

Bite. Swallow. 'OK.'

'Definitely a hunk,' Lizzie said, trying not to notice that the plate was now half-empty. This was better than Lillian had done all week. 'If he wasn't in a wheelchair and engaged to Emily, I definitely wouldn't be sharing a house with him. No way.'

'He's a bit wasted on Emily.' Lillian thought about it for a bit longer. 'Though he is quite old.'

'Yeah, gee, he must be at least thirty-two or three. One foot in the grave, so to speak. It's a wonder he still has the energy to get married.'

Lillian chuckled and to Lizzie's absolute delight she raised a forkful of peas without thinking. And swallowed all by herself. 'Well, he is quite well preserved for your generation,' she said, and Lizzie smiled even more.

'My generation. Thanks very much.'

Lillian refused to hear the huffiness. She saw the smile and she was intent on Dr McKay's love life.

'Emily's really boring,' she told her. 'She's been here for ever. When Dr McKay's fiancée was killed…'

'Dr McKay's fiancée was killed?'

'Ages ago. When I was about ten. Mum said Emily meant to have him then. She was so nice and they've just sort of been a pair ever since. Mum says they got engaged without Dr McKay even noticing and it was only when he was about to be married that he panicked.'

'He panicked?'

'That's what everyone said. Why else would he have hit your car?'

'You know, if I was going to commit suicide I might have chosen a better method than throwing myself under a tiny, tinpot hire car that was travelling less than ten miles an hour.'

'I don't think he was committing suicide.'

She should stop this conversation. She should stop it right now. But Lillian's food was going down—the plate was well over half-demolished now. To haul her away from gossip would be criminal.

'Besides…'

Besides nothing, she told herself. She was doing this as a doctor reacting to medical need. Nothing more.

'Besides what?'

'Well, suicide would be silly,' Lillian said. 'This town needs him. Everyone says so. If he suicided then Birrini wouldn't have a doctor.'

'I guess not.' There wasn't an answer to that. Next time she was feeling like reaching for the pills she hoped that there was someone around to remind her that she was irreplaceable. Even if it was just as a family doctor…

But maybe there was a real risk of suicide. 'Mum says Emily and her mother have talked nothing but bridesmaids' dresses for a year,' Lillian told her. 'She was having six bridesmaids and two flower girls. It was gonna be amazing.'

'I guess it still will be amazing.'

'If he goes through with it.'

'Why shouldn't he go through with it?'

'Because he's living with you.'

'Hey!'

Enough. Lillian had eaten enough, and this conversation was getting entirely out of hand. She rose and rang the bell and managed an uncertain smile down at Lillian. Moving right on...

'That was great, Lillian. You've eaten about half of what I intend to eat tonight. It was a really good dinner.'

'Don't ring the bell,' Lillian told her. 'I'll be fine by myself. I won't make myself sick.'

She would. Of course she would. Lizzie had succeeded in distracting her enough to make her eat, but that was the easy part. The hard bit was keeping it down.

'Sorry, Lillian, but you know the deal.'

'Don't you trust me?'

'No.'

Lillian gave her a reluctant smile. 'Oh, well...' She shrugged. 'If you're going to be picky.'

'I'm going to be picky.' She touched Lillian lightly on the cheek. 'I can almost see dimples, my girl. We're succeeding. So you're going to keep right on eating—and holding it down—until you have boobs almost as cuddly as mine.'

Lillian sighed. 'You can't stay, can you?' she asked wistfully. 'I hate Mrs Pround.'

Mrs Pround was the ward assistant. She wasn't an ideal companion for a fifteen-year-old, but she had the huge advantage of having eyes like a gimlet. Lillian would never get her fingers down her throat to make herself sick while Mrs Pround was in a half-mile radius. She wouldn't dare.

But Lizzie was already backing out the door. 'I'm sorry, Lillian, but I have a ward round to do before I find my own dinner,' she told her. 'I need to go.'

'Will I do instead?'

The door swung wide and Harry McKay and his wheelchair rolled smoothly to the bedside.

'Um…how long have you been outside the room?'

As a greeting it was a dead give-away, but it was all Lizzie could think of.

'And why aren't you on your crutches?' she demanded, and he gave her a crooked grin.

'The wheelchair is quieter. I can get places without being noticed.'

'You heard?'

'Obviously.'

'But...I said that about your fiancée.' Lillian had clearly replayed their conversation really fast and the teenager was already feeling mortified. She was looking at Harry and her fragile self-confidence was crumbling while they watched. 'I said... Oh, I'm so sorry.'

'Hey, I heard you two discussing what a hunk I was,' Harry told her, and puffed out his chest. 'Very nice.'

'But we—'

'And I also heard you discuss boob enlargement. Even nicer.'

'Will you cut it out?' Lizzie was laughing. She picked up a magazine from the tray top and swiped him over the ear. 'Eavesdroppers never hear any good of themselves.'

'I'm not an eavesdropper,' he said, wounded. 'I just had to lean against the door to rest.'

'Right. You sat in your wheelchair and leaned.'

'My right shoulder still carries the dent. Want to see?'

'I'd probably see the shape of the doorknob indented in your right ear,' she retorted.

'We said—' Lillian whispered, but Lizzie was having none of it.

'We were discussing how old he was,' she said. 'So old he's practically incapable of getting himself married. Which is why he bumped into my car. His sight must be fading, poor dear.'

'Say it louder, girlie,' Harry flashed. 'My ear trumpet seems to have been mislaid. And I've mislaid my leg. I'll lose my nose any minute. Come to think of it...' He squinted. 'Where is my nose?'

'Sticking into places it has no right to be,' Lizzie told him, trying not to laugh. She glared and fixed him with a look that said she knew very well he'd heard everything and he'd better watch himself. 'Are you intending to stay with Lillian?'

'I brought the Monopoly board.'

'What do you reckon, Lillian? Can you face playing Monopoly with a man in his dotage?'

And thankfully—blessedly—Lillian was chuckling.

'Well, there you go, then.' Lizzie left them to it, but as she made her way down the corridor to the patients who were waiting for her, she was aware of a sharp stab of regret.

Monopoly. It was a game she'd never enjoyed.

But tonight she really felt like playing.

*　　*　　*

There were three casseroles and an enormous trout on the kitchen table when Lizzie walked through to the doctor's residence two hours later. Phoebe was right underneath, gazing upward with hope.

Harry was balancing on crutches. He was wearing a pink frilly apron and he was wielding a filleting knife.

She stopped dead.

'Don't move,' she said faintly. 'Don't do it.'

He looked up from his trout, bemused. 'Sorry?'

'You're not fit for surgery. The fish can keep his appendix. Put down the knife, Dr McKay, and move back from the table slowly.'

He grinned. 'Are you implying I'm a lunatic?'

'Implying? No. Saying you are? Definitely.'

'I'm perfectly capable of filleting a fish.'

'Right. Like you're perfectly capable of standing upright. All you need to do is overbalance and Phoebe gets it.'

'So it's concern for your basset.'

'Of course.' She walked forward and lifted the knife from his fingers before he could protest. She moved out of range, holding the knife behind her back.

'Give me back my knife,' he told her, glowering. 'I'm fine.'

'You're wearing a pink apron.'

'That doesn't necessarily mean I'm deranged.'

'You're a sick man, Dr McKay.'

He glared at her, baulked, and she laughed.

Where had this laughter come from? she thought. It had sprung up, unbidden, a constant in their relationship that refused to go away.

'I'm warning you...'

'Or what?' Her eyes danced. From under the table Phoebe gazed from one to the other with an expression that said she was really confused. But hopeful.

So what was new? Phoebe was permanently confused—and hopeful. Where food was concerned. She barked and emerged from under the table, trying her best to jump up on Harry's combination of legs and crutches. It didn't work. Jumping up for Phoebe meant getting her front legs three inches above the ground.

'You traitor,' Lizzie told her. 'Leave him alone. The man is a knife-wielder, Phoebe. Come to Mummy.'

'The man doesn't have a knife. Mummy has the knife.'

'So she does.'

'Give it back.'

'Don't be a dodo.'

'Is that your very best crisis counselling skill?'

'Yes.'

'It'll lead to a confrontation.' With laughter deepening around his eyes, he leaned over and lifted the trout. 'OK, Dr Darling, you asked for it.' The trout was raised right over Phoebe's head. 'Give me my filleting knife or the puppy gets it.'

She choked on laughter at that—and at the expression of pure hope in Phoebe's mournful basset eyes. 'The puppy would love it.'

'What, a whole trout?'

'And the rest. Honestly, Harry, you're not stable and you know it. You can't fillet. You shouldn't even be standing up. Let's eat one of these casseroles.'

'When we can eat trout? No way.'

'Then teach me to fillet,' she told him.

He looked at her, considering. 'Really?'

'Really. If I can wear the pink pinny.'

'I've got two. You're on.'

The time spent cleaning and stuffing the fish was probably one of the silliest half-hours she'd ever spent in her life. Dressed in his frilly apron,

Harry turned into 'Professor of Anatomy—Fish' and proceeded to guide her though the incredibly delicate operation of preparing one trout for consumption.

'I'm sure fishermen don't go to this trouble,' she protested, but he shook his head.

'No. Of course not, but we're not fishermen, Dr Darling. We're surgeons.'

'Speak for yourself.'

'Well, I'm a surgeon,' he told her. 'You will be as soon as you conquer gills.'

'You're a surgeon?'

'Mmm.' He seemed almost embarrassed.

'A qualified surgeon?'

'Yes. There's some scales—'

But she was distracted. 'What's a surgeon doing here? In Birrini.'

'Practising medicine. Watch your scales, Dr Darling.'

'But you don't have an anaesthetist.'

'Good noticing.'

'So you practise your surgery on awake patients?'

'I don't practise surgery at all.' All of a sudden the laughter left his eyes and she looked up at him in concern.

'Then why are you here? In Birrini?'

'I want to be here,' he told her, his voice clipped and strained. 'Now…back to the fish.'

She could take a hint. He wanted the subject changed. Don't probe, his voice had said, and she was a champion at not probing. Though there were some questions that had to be asked.

'Tell me where you got these aprons,' she begged, and the laughter flashed back again. It was the way he liked it, she thought. Light and shallow. Frilly apron shallow.

'Emily was given six aprons at her hens' night. Six different colours. All with frills. No one gave me anything as cool as that at my bachelor do. I couldn't resist.'

'She gave them to you?'

'I pinched some,' he told her. 'I didn't see why such fine couturier fashions should be the domain of women only.'

'Emily knows you're wearing them?'

'Emily doesn't know the half of it,' he told her, and then under his breath he added a rider. 'Thank God.'

The trout was delicious. So was the vegetable casserole they had with it and the rhubarb pie that appeared just as they were clearing the dishes. The elderly man who arrived on the back porch bearing the pie beamed at the pair of them as they opened the screen door to greet him.

'Mabel said you'd maybe appreciate this seeing the doctor's off his leg.' He produced a ham bone as well. 'And this is for the pooch. Goodnight to the pair of you.' And he disappeared as swiftly as he'd come. Birrini hospitality. Amazing!

Even Phoebe was impressed. Lizzie's dog was practically beaming with contentment. She lay on the porch and slobbered over her bone and Harry ate his pie and looked out at her with wonder.

'Phoebe was your grandma's dog?'

'Yep.'

'She's not exactly a suitable dog for an old lady.'

'My grandma wasn't exactly a suitable old lady,' Lizzie told him, smiling at the memory of the old lady she'd loved. 'Grandma was a palaeontologist. World renowned.'

'A…a what?'

'A palaeontologist. She studied dinosaurs. Grandma spent her time travelling the world, collecting bones. It was only the last few years of her life that she was stuck in Australia. So Phoebe became the love of her declining years.'

'Which explains Phoebe's love of bones.' Harry grinned at Phoebe who was attacking the ham bone like all her Christmases had come at once.

Lizzie smiled, but she was still thinking about Grandma. The old lady's death was still raw in her heart, and it was good to talk about her. 'Grandma's bones were generally a whole lot older than this one,' she told him. 'I spent my childhood dusting and sorting and figuring out which bone went where. Maybe that's why I became a doctor.'

He was watching her across the table, his face curious. 'You lived with your grandma?'

'I went to boarding school while she travelled. But, yes, I lived with her.'

'Where were your parents?'

'They were killed in a light plane crash when I was seven. I can barely remember them, but what I can...they were great. I loved them very much. That's why I can't change my name.'

'You'd change it if you could?'

'It's a bit hard,' she admitted, 'to go through your life being a Darling.'

'I guess it must be.'

'And you?' she asked, and Harry looked a question. 'Tell me about you. Where are your parents?'

'Sorry?'

'They weren't here for the wedding,' she said. 'At least, they weren't here when you were injured. You mostly seemed to be surrounded by Emily's family.'

'I don't have a family.'

'They're dead?'

'I just don't have a family.'

That was all he was telling her. They finished eating and then she shooed him outside to sit on the porch while she did the dishes. He protested, but she was adamant. As she cleaned up the kitchen she was aware of him—watching her.

What was it with him? When she'd first met him she'd thought of him as a carefree young family doctor about to be married. Now...there were depths, she thought. Shadows.

She shouldn't probe. She should let him be. As soon as Phoebe had her pups she'd be out of here, and this man and the little community he cared for would mean nothing to her any longer.

Don't get involved. That's what her heart was screaming, but she wasn't listening. She finished cleaning and then walked outside to join him.

'Aren't you cold?' The night was clear and crisp. From the back porch you could see right across the little township down to the sea beyond. The sea was almost half a mile from here, but the moon was full and a ghostly sheen was washing over the waves.

Beautiful.

'I'm not thinking of cold,' Harry told her. 'I'm thinking I'm really pleased to be back home.'

'It's not much fun being in hospital.'

'It's not much fun being in the city.'

She looked at him curiously but he was a million miles away. He'd propped his crutches by the rail and had sunk down onto an ancient cane settee. He didn't look the successful young doctor now, she thought. He'd discarded the apron—thankfully. He was in his shorts and battered sweatshirt and his leg with the brace on was resting on a stool in front of him. But it was more than his clothes and his injured leg, she thought. He was gazing out at the sea and his whole demeanour... The way his eyes creased as they gazed out into the distance. The lines at the corners of his eyes. The way his hair was tousled and casual and...

'You look more like a farmer than a doctor,' she told him, and he looked up at her, startled.

'Why do you say that?'

'I don't know. You're just...at home, I suppose.'

'I am,' he said softly. He gazed out at the bushland and the lights of the tiny town between here and the sea. 'I tried the city once but it's a dog's life.' Then, as Phoebe stirred and wuffled at his feet, he smiled and put a hand down to stroke her floppy ears. 'OK, Phoebe. I wouldn't condemn a basset to it either.'

'Hey, the city's not so bad.'

'You've always lived there?'

'Mmm.'

'You should try this.'

'I thought that's just what I was doing,' she said cautiously, sitting herself down beside him and staring seaward as well.

'But you'll leave.'

'Of course I'll leave. When have you re-scheduled the wedding?'

'We haven't yet.'

Lizzie thought about that. 'I'd imagine Emily would be anxious.'

'Mmm.'

She frowned. 'You are still getting married?'

He stared out to sea. 'Yeah. Yeah, of course we are.'

'Harry?'

'Yes?'

'Um…is there anything you're not telling me?'

'Nope.'

'I think I have the right to know,' she said. 'I was employed as a locum while you were on your honeymoon. Do you still want me to stay?'

'Of course.'

'There's no "of course" about it. I can't stay here indefinitely.'

'Yes, there is. When are Phoebe's puppies due?'

'In two or three weeks.'

'You can't leave before they're born.'

'No, but—'

'And you can't leave while you have new-borns. I'm sure your obstetrician would advise against it. That's two weeks before birth and six or eight weeks with puppies. It should give me time to get back on my feet.'

'And have a honeymoon?'

'Maybe.'

She thought about it. It was the strangest night. She was sitting on the back porch with a man she hardly knew, yet the setting was so intimate that she felt like she'd known him all her life.

She certainly hadn't!

She slid off the settee onto the floorboards. Phoebe slithered forward over her knees and pushed her big head up under Lizzie's hands, searching for a scratch. Out in the bush a mo-poke was calling, slow and mournful.

She didn't feel mournful, she thought. She felt at peace.

'I didn't mean to slam into your car,' Harry said softly, and she turned to stare up at him.

'I didn't think you did,' she told him. 'I can think of surer ways to commit suicide. And, besides, I've met Emily. There's no need for a man to take drastic steps there.'

He gave a half-hearted smile. 'I was just... distracted.'

'Six bridesmaids and two flower girls would be enough to distract anyone.'

'I guess.' He gazed some more and she scratched Phoebe some more. It was the strangest feeling. Peace... Like she'd found her home.

Nonsense. Her home was in Queensland. With Edward?

No and no and no. She hugged Phoebe close—which was sort of like hugging a sack of warmed jello. But it was the comfort she needed.

There were fingers touching her hair.

'Why are you here?' he asked, and she turned toward him in surprise. His hand stayed on her head, drifting through her curls.

'I told you.'

'You told me you're here for your dog. It doesn't make sense.'

'It does make sense.' She strove really hard to ignore the feel of those fingers drifting along her forehead. She was seated at his feet. It was a gesture of warmth—a touch that meant nothing. Her hair was right under his hands and it was the easiest thing to touch her as he asked his question. It meant nothing...

The fact that it sent slivers of warmth to every corner of her body was immaterial. Immaterial nonsense. It meant nothing.

Nothing...

'I told you,' she said. 'Airlines don't carry pregnant dogs.'

'Right.' The fingers paused and then moved on and it was as much as she could do not to move her head under his hand, cat-like, so he could reach every spot. He was actually doing a fine job of reaching every spot without her moving. 'So the airlines do a pregnancy test on every dog as they crate them? I don't think so.'

'She looks pregnant.'

'She looks fat.'

'Hey!'

'It's true,' he told her firmly. 'If I had to say whether Phoebe was pregnant or fat, I know which I'd choose.'

'That's not very nice.'

'No, but it's honest. And the flight from here to Cairns is three hours. Hardly time to divert the plane for an emergency basset Caesarean.'

'You're telling me I'm a liar?'

'Nope. I'm asking why you're really down here.'

'It's none of your business.'

'Right.' He considered. 'But you'll stay on for a while?'

'It was supposed to be for three weeks.'

'I need you for longer than that.'

Those fingers were driving her crazy. She was practically purring. Three weeks...three weeks of sitting out on the back porch and having this man rub his fingers through her hair...

Three weeks wasn't long enough, she thought.

What would she tell Edward?

Family business. It was a complex matter, settling her grandma's affairs. The hospital she worked for would understand. They'd just welcomed their new intake of interns for the year and included was an overseas trained doctor who'd done ten years' emergency medicine in South Africa. He'd needed the job as intern to get his Australian registration, but he was seriously good. The hospital would barely miss Lizzie for the next few weeks.

So she could stay. If Harry kept moving his fingers through her hair.

It was ridiculous. Harry was engaged to Emily. She shouldn't be feeling like this.

She was.

'Um…I can stay,' she murmured. The night was getting away from her. The whole situation had assumed a dream-like quality. The way his fingers moved… It was almost hypnotic. Wonderful.

'Do you want me to remove your back-slab and give your leg a rub?' she managed. 'I… The notes. They said the leg needed to be rubbed.'

'I don't think that'd be wise,' he told her, and his voice was suddenly so unsteady that she thought, He's feeling exactly the same way I am. 'Do you?'

'You need the circulation kept going. I don't want deep vein thrombosis.'

'No, I don't. But neither do I want any other complications.'

Right. They both knew what he was talking about. The fingers ceased their stroking and Lizzie hauled herself away. Phoebe cast her a baleful glare and Lizzie thought, Yeah, I know just how you feel. Deprived.

She hauled herself to her feet and looked down uncertainly at Harry in the moonlight.

'Do you want a cup of tea?'

'That'd be great.'

Distance. They were carefully putting distance between them. Building a barricade that was fragile, but it was the best they could do.

'I'll go, then.'

'Right.'

But Lizzie didn't move. She stood there, staring.

The phone rang. Thankfully—because otherwise she would have stood there all night. She didn't want to move an inch.

He was engaged to Emily.

She had Edward.

She gave herself a fierce inward shake and went to answer the phone.

CHAPTER FIVE

Memo:
I will not go and see what the trouble is.
Lizzie is a fine doctor. I need to stay off my
feet, If I make myself useful then she might
not stay.

I will not think about Lizzie staying.

I will go and ring Emily and tell her...tell
her... Tell her what?

I will not ring Emily.

I will not go and see what the trouble is.
Good doctors do not interfere with another
good doctor's work.

I will just make sure...

TROUBLE.

Lizzie could hear a child sobbing in pain as soon as she swung open the dividing door into Emergency. May met her, looking concerned.

'Aren't you supposed to be off duty?' she asked, and the nurse shook her head.

'One of the other girls has flu. With Emily away we're tight. I'm working split shift till midnight. And I know Terry.'

'Terry?'

'He's a friend of one of my kids. His parents are farmers. Sensible folk.' She glanced over to a cubicle where the child was rocking back and forth on the bed with his father trying to hold him down. 'Um...you should know that they're a bit puritan. Or very puritan. They won't even tell me what's wrong. They want Harry to see the boy—because he's a man, I gather, and what's wrong with Terry is a man's problem.'

'He's how old?'

'Eleven.'

'Man's problem. Right.' Lizzie unconsciously braced herself. Problems like this happened all the time in a big city emergency department. Problems out of left field. Like the biker who refused to be treated unless he could keep his pit bull terrier under his jacket all the time—a bit of a problem when she needed to take X-rays. Or the parent who refused to let go of a baby when the child needed resuscitation.

Problems. She could handle problems.

'Is Harry awake?' May asked, and she shook her head.

'He might be awake but he's not working to-night. He's a patient himself.'

'But—'

'Come on, May,' she said, grinning. 'We can handle this. What's a mere man's problem for two competent women?' She pinned her efficient, doctor-in-charge-of-the-world smile on her face, shrugged on the white coat that May was holding out to her and walked over to the bed.

The parents seemed to unconsciously stiffen. There was no welcome at all.

'Hi,' she told them. 'I'm Dr Lizzie Darling. I'm looking after Dr McKay's patients while he's ill. What seems to be the problem?'

They didn't reply. The man held his son tighter and the woman sank down onto a bedside chair and wept. They both looked away from her. Then the child whimpered in his father's arms and clutched his groin. He doubled over and his face was bleached white.

'Where's Dr McKay?' the farmer growled, but Lizzie had seen enough. A hurting child wasn't to be put aside because his parents were worried about which doctor they wanted. She sat on the bed beside the farmer and moved to prise the little boy's hands away from his groin.

'Terry, let me see what the matter is. I'm a doctor. I can help.'

'It's his... You can't...' his mother whispered, but enough was enough.

'I'm a qualified doctor,' she told them, her voice stern. 'I've treated hundreds of children in my time in medical practice. There's nothing here to shock me, and I'm not interfering with Terry's privacy. Terry, I need to examine you. I can't stop the pain unless I know what's wrong.'

His parents looked wildly at each other. Terry whimpered again and started to sob. Lizzie signalled to May. The nurse moved in, took the farmer's hand and propelled him forward.

'Let Dr Darling see what's happening,' she said. 'She's good. Don't hold her up.'

The farmer moved a whole six inches back.

For heaven's sake. What was their problem? This wasn't something like a blood transfusion, Lizzie thought, where religious beliefs might be an issue. It was pure and stupid coyness.

Coyness or not, Terry had been inculcated with his parents' obsession for decency. The little boy was clutching the front of his pyjama pants and he was looking up at her in pure terror.

'What is it, Terry?'

'It hurts,' he whispered. He threw a scared look at his parents, as if expecting punishment, but his need for help was overriding what he'd been taught. 'Me...me balls...'

His testicles.

Lizzie nodded. It was what she'd been starting to expect. Terry was the right age for this sort of problem.

But the easy things had to be excluded first. 'Have you had an infection?' she asked. 'Has it been sore down there for a while?'

'No. Only tonight. After dinner.' He gave another moan and clutched himself again.

'I need to see, Terry.'

'But…you're a girl.' Another look at his parents and what he saw there seemed to cement his conviction as to what was right and what was absolutely wrong. He clutched himself even tighter. It was apparent to everyone that his dignity was more important than his need for assistance.

He looked up at her wildly and Lizzie knew if she touched him she'd spark hysteria. Maybe from all of them.

Now what? Lizzie took a deep breath. 'Look, this is foolish—'

'Can I help?'

Harry.

She turned and Harry was right behind her, balancing on his crutches in the doorway. What was he doing here? She cast him a glance that was half exasperated, half relieved.

'We have a bad case of sex discrimination here,' she told him, and he nodded. He'd been listening for a while, then.

'And now's not the time to take it to the equal opportunity commissioner?' His eyes were smiling at her, and she thought suddenly, Great. It was great that he was here.

She didn't need him. She shouldn't.

But it was great.

'Stand back and let me see,' he told her, so she did just that while Harry bent over the little boy. To her indignation there wasn't the slightest hesitation in the child agreeing to let Harry see.

'You know, Dr Lizzie's not really a girl,' Harry told the little boy as he adjusted the child's pyjamas. 'She's a doctor. For future reference, I think you and your parents need to figure out the difference. But for now I can look after you.'

Lizzie's not really a girl...

'Hey,' Lizzie said indignantly from behind him. 'I like being a girl.'

'Stethoscope or pantyhose, take your pick.' He gave her a grin over his shoulder. He was leaning heavily on the bed, and she moved to take his crutches before they toppled. 'It seems in Terry's terms you can't have both.'

She hesitated. That grin had the power to deflect her but some things were important. The crutches were in her hands now. They should be in his. She glared. 'What do you think you're doing?' she demanded. 'You can't stand up.'

'I'm a one-legged wonder. It's time you realised that. Now, Dr Darling, turn your face to the wall and let Terry and me get on with secret men's business.'

Turn your face to the wall? She swallowed and glared some more, but he was no longer paying her attention. All his attention was on Terry. Lizzie and May were left to talk to themselves.

Even the parents had turned away. Some people took privacy to absurd levels, Lizzie thought. To raise a child with this level of paranoia about personal privacy was asking for trouble.

At least Harry was here. She could have managed this, she thought. She could.

But it was just as well Harry was here.

There was silence during the examination. Terry had stopped whimpering and the parents were shocked and speechless. Waiting for the worst.

Had they looked themselves? By the appearance of fear on their faces, they seemed to think it could be anything that Harry was finding down there. Good grief.

'I wonder if they changed his nappies when he was a baby?' May whispered behind her hand, and Lizzie shushed her but then had to choke back a giggle.

She was a doctor. Not a girl. She had to remember that.

'There's no sign of infection,' Harry said at last. 'But it's really tender. I need to do a test for a urinary tract infection. Can we get a sample?'

'I guess we can if you hold the bottle,' Lizzie told him. 'I bet that's men's business as well.' May snorted, turned it into a cough and caught her eye, and suddenly the two women were grinning at each other like fools.

Or like…friends?

Where had that thought come from? Lizzie wondered, but it consolidated. Here in this little room with this rigid farming family, with the caring doctor with the gammy leg and the kindly smile, with the laughing nurse sharing a joke…

She could stay here.

Now, there was another crazy thought. She had no business thinking about long-term plans when she should be concentrating on the needs of an ill child. But there was little to concentrate on when it was Harry who had to cope with obtaining a urine sample.

'I'll fetch the bottle,' May said, and Lizzie stepped out of the room as well so that she could do her grinning in private.

'Collecting urine samples isn't our Dr McKay's favourite job, but serve him right,' May muttered, once the bottle had been handed over. While this intensely personal operation was going on there was nothing they could do but wait. 'Men. Do you think you and I should retire to the kitchen and do a little knitting, Dr Darling?'

'Could you run the tests?' Harry asked, and handed the bottle through the door. He looked from Lizzie to May and back again and added. 'Please?'

'See?' May said darkly. 'Running tests on little bottles of urine. That counts as cooking. Women's work. Keep them barefoot and pregnant…'

'And in the lab where they belong.' Lizzie grinned and took the bottle from Harry. As she turned toward the lab she was aware of him watching her.

He watched her all the way down the corridor and May watched him.

Well, well, well.

*   *   *

'There's no sign of infection.'

Minutes later Lizzie had the results of the urine sample test. 'Nothing,' she told him.

Harry parked his crutches and sank into a chair in the nurses' station. 'The tenderness is getting worse.'

'Torsion?'

'It has to be.'

They stared at each other. The laughter of a few minutes ago had disappeared. Each knew what was happening.

In boys this age it could occur out of the blue—a twisting of the testes inside the scrotum. Left alone, the testis would lose all blood supply and would die.

The only way to manage the problem was to operate. Now.

'You're not up to operating,' she told him.

'The alternative is sending him to Melbourne, but by the time he reaches Melbourne the damage will have been done. He's risking the loss of his testicle. There are implications for long-term fertility. We need to move.'

Lizzie swallowed. 'He may already... The damage may already be irreversible.'

'He's only been in real pain for twenty minutes. If we move fast...'

'You can't.'

'Of course I can. I'll get a stool set up in Theatre. It's a simple operation and I assume you can give an anaesthetic.'

'For something like this? Of course I can.'

'Then what are we waiting for?'

'I'm a woman,' she told him, making her voice meek. 'You think I should be allowed in the operating suite?'

'We'll rig up a sheet,' he told her, his eyes creasing again with the laughter she was starting to love. 'We wouldn't want to shock our Dr Darling, now, would we?'

It was a straightforward operation, for which Lizzie was profoundly grateful. Despite his protestations, Harry was starting to look distinctly grey around the edges. It had been a long trip back by ambulance, even if he had been able to lie down. He was six days post-trauma and his body was still not close to recovered.

'I'm fine,' he growled as he saw her watching him. 'Concentrate on your anaesthetic.'

'Yes, sir.' She adjusted the mask on the little boy's face and turned back to her monitors. He'd gone to sleep without any problem at all. There'd been no more hassle with either Terry himself or his parents—it seemed that once he was asleep Lizzie could be a doctor and not a female.

The anaesthetic was textbook simple. Terry was a healthy little eleven-year-old with no problems other that the one Harry was intent on fixing. She could afford to let her attention divide a little so that she could watch Harry.

The man was seriously skilled. His fingers were swift and nimble, not hesitating in the least. He swabbed the area, draped and made a neat incision, wincing as he saw what lay exposed.

'Poor kid. No wonder he's been complaining. If this happened to me I'd be climbing walls.'

'Twisted?'

'The testis has turned inside the scrotum. Hell. There's no blood getting through at all.'

Silence. It was a tricky little procedure, manoeuvring it back.

Harry's fingers were gently shifting, moving the testis into a more natural position, enabling the blood vessels to work…

'Ah…'

The theatre—collectively Lizzie and May—held its breath.

'Ah?' Lizzie said.

'Colour.'

Colour. She knew what he meant.

OK, for many men one damaged testicle didn't mean infertility, but often it did. To condemn an eleven-year-old to a lifetime prospect of never becoming a dad...

'It's even better than your leg,' she said in quiet satisfaction, and he cast a startled glance up at her.

'Hey. We're talking infertility here. That's a darn sight less important than losing a leg.'

'Is it?' She frowned, still concentrating on her dials.

Harry appeared to think about it. He was starting to stitch, fastening the testis to the wall of the scrotum so it couldn't twist again.

'I reckon.' He told her. 'Babies or leg? No choice really.'

'I bet Emily wouldn't think so,' May retorted, and Harry gave a rueful grin.

'That's because it's not Emily's leg.'

'You wouldn't give up your leg for a baby?' Lizzie asked curiously.

'Well, I might have to,' he conceded. 'I mean, if you held up a living, breathing baby called Alphonse and you said to me, "Your leg or the baby gets it," then maybe I'd concede a leg.'

'Gee, that's good of you.'

'Alphonse would have to be a very nice baby as well.'

'Emily wants six babies,' May volunteered, and Harry nearly dropped his needle. He caught himself and concentrated harder, and Lizzie grinned.

'That's not a good thing to drop on an operating surgeon, Sister,' she told May. 'We could have him faint in Theatre and then where would we be?'

'He's just doing needlework now,' May retorted but she looked a little abashed. 'I could do that.'

'Yeah right,' Harry said. He stitched some more. 'Six babies?' he asked cautiously, and May nodded.

'That's what she said. Though I concede that maybe I shouldn't be the one to break it to you. I think you need to speak to your bride.'

'Phoebe's likely to have six babies or maybe even more,' Lizzie volunteered. All of a sudden the grey tinge on Harry's face had become more pronounced and she was starting to worry. He should be in bed. All she could do was lighten things up and hope.

'Can we award six art prizes?' May asked. Like Lizzie, she'd seen the strain descend on Harry's face and she was prepared to take a lead.

'Nope. I'll leave the other five with our Dr McKay. If Emily wants six babies, that's five of Phoebe's and if he and Emily try really hard and read all the proper instruction manuals then maybe they can make one all of their own. Their own little Alphonse who they won't even have to sacrifice a leg to obtain.'

He should smile, she thought. The laughter should come back. But it wasn't appearing.

'Dressing,' he said curtly, and May handed him what he needed with a curious sideways glance at Lizzie.

They'd stepped over a boundary. They knew it. But neither of them knew exactly what that boundary was.

With the anaesthetic reversed and Terry slowly and drowsily coming around to the land of the living, and with his parents reassured, it was time to call it quits. Harry made his way through to the doctor's quarters, leaning heavily on his elbow crutches, and Lizzie followed in concern.

'Let me help you get into bed,' she said, but he shook his head.

'I can do it.'

'I'm a doctor, remember?' she said gently. 'You're not going to do a Terry on me, are you?'

'No, but—'

'If I leave you alone you're just going to flop down on your bed and sleep just as you are— aren't you?'

'How do you know?'

'I can see it in your face.'

'You can see too damned much,' he said enigmatically, but she was already holding the bedroom door for him.

'In. Now. Sit on the bed and let me help you undress.'

'I can—'

'You can't. Sit. Submit to being cared for. Now.'

It shouldn't be personal.

She was a doctor, and he, for the moment, was a patient. How many times in her medical practice had she helped a patient undress? Hundreds, she thought.

It was stupid to avoid this. Harry knew it too. He left his boxers on—a man had some pride— but he let her slip the rest of his clothes from his body and pull on a pyjama jacket. Then he slid back onto the sheets with a sigh of relief and watched as she examined his leg.

'Is it hurting?'

'Like hell,' he admitted.

'You shouldn't have been on it.'

'I hardly had a choice.'

No. Terry would have been in real trouble without him.

'Can you bear for me to give it a rub?' she told him. 'I swear I'll be gentle.'

'It doesn't need it.'

'You know it does,' she told him. 'I didn't do all that heroic leg manipulation in the pouring rain only to have my patient die of deep vein thrombosis.'

'I'm not intending to develop DVT.'

'Not if you let me massage it,' she said demurely. 'Come on, Dr McKay. Let the nice doctor do her job. I promise you it'll barely tickle.'

'Liar,' he said, and she chuckled.

'Be brave, then,' she told him. 'If you're very good I'll see if I can find you a jelly bean from the kids' ward as a reward.'

Under the bandages the leg still looked swollen and painful. Lizzie laid the last of the bandages aside and winced.

'Ouch.'

'Hey, who has to be brave here?'

'Sorry.' She pulled up a chair and sat, making a careful assessment of the wound.

The leg had been broken two thirds of the distance from knee to ankle. The plate and pin had been inserted through a neat incision that would heal really well.

'You'll be as good as new in no time,' she said appreciatively. 'That's a very nice scar.'

'Why, thank you.' He had his hands linked behind his head and was staring up at the ceiling.

'If it hurts you, I'll stop,' she said gently, and he glared.

'I'm not scared.'

'I'd be scared if I were you,' she told him. 'Letting me practise my massage skills on you. I'd be scared out of my wits.'

But she didn't hurt him.

Lizzie had watched the physiotherapists in the orthopaedic wards enough to do no harm now, and to achieve what she wanted. Carefully, skilfully she massaged the swollen leg, keeping well clear of the wound itself. She left the backslab on, slipping her slender fingers under when she wanted to gain purchase. She didn't want to encourage movement at this stage. She simply wanted to facilitate the blood supply through the bruised and damaged blood vessels. And ease the hurt.

She took her time. Slowly stroking. Kneading. Over and over, gently and soothingly, taking all the time in the world.

She didn't speak, and he didn't seem to want to either. She simply moved her fingers carefully over his bruised leg, letting him lie back on the pillows with his thoughts going where they willed.

And somehow—some time—the tension faded from Harry's face. The lines of pain and the tinge of grey eased and faded.

It felt good, she decided. Great. Maybe she should have been a masseuse instead of a doctor. To have the capacity to wipe away pain.

From this man's face…

He was just a patient, she told herself. Just a patient.

'You work in Emergency up north?' he asked, and the question was a jolt all by itself. She had been far away, but she hadn't been thinking of work. She hadn't been thinking of home.

'Mmm.'

'Nine to five?'

'Eight to four or four to midnight or midnight to eight,' she told him, still massaging the tightness of his calf muscles.

'And you walk away afterwards?'

'There's not a lot of follow-up in emergency medicine.' She shrugged. 'Sometimes I get involved. I can't help it. But not often.'

'You don't like getting involved?'

'Not if I can help it.'

He was watching her, those deep eyes calmly speculative. It seemed he'd relaxed at last, and as he relaxed he could think about her. She wasn't sure she liked it.

'Why don't you like getting involved?'

Lizzie sighed. She looked at him but his eyes were nonjudgmental. They were asking a question. She could tell him to butt out of what wasn't his business, but all of a sudden... It wouldn't hurt to tell him. This hurtful thing.

'When I was a newly qualified doctor I did a stint in family practice,' she told him. She was concentrating on his leg again, carefully not looking at him. 'I had a kid come to me with depression. She was fifteen years old. About the same age as Lillian. Anyway, I was a know-it-all, just graduated family doctor. I read up all the literature on antidepressants. I practised my counselling skills. I tried family therapy with Patti as well as her parents. All the things we were taught as bright little potential doctors.' She bit her lip and the fingers massaging Harry's leg stilled. Remembering hurt.

'And?' he said softly, but by the sound of his tone he knew what was coming.

'You know,' she told him. 'It's not hard to guess. Patti was trying so hard to please me. ''Of course I feel better,'' she told me. ''I feel great.'' The night after she told me that she took a massive overdose of every medicine she could find in the house and she was dead before anyone found her.'

'Tough,' Harry murmured, and Lizzie swallowed.

'It was. So, you see, I'm not all that clever. I figured that playing expert is a fool's game. So now I see patients at the coalface—in Emergency. I patch them up as best I can and then I refer them on to people who really know their stuff.'

'You think Patti would still be alive if you hadn't treated her?'

'If she'd seen a skilled psychiatrist...'

'Would she have gone to see a psychiatrist?' Harry's eyes were resting on her face, unsettling her with what he seemed to be seeing. 'Lillian won't see a psychiatrist. She refuses, and her parents back her up. Do you think I should refuse to treat her because of that?'

'No, I—'

'There are all sorts of people in Birrini who should be seeing specialists,' he continued. 'They're not. They don't want to take the trip to the city. Or they don't trust people they don't know. They make the decision to keep their lives in my hands. And if I occasionally lose one of those lives...'

'You wouldn't.'

'I do,' he said wearily. 'Of course I do. I had an old man die three weeks ago because he refused to go to Melbourne for bypass surgery. I tried to keep him alive here, but I didn't have the skills. Does that make me want to walk away?'

She flushed. 'You think I'm a coward?'

'I know you're not.'

Silence.

The silence went on and on. And in that silence something built. Something intangible. Something neither of them recognised, but it was there for all that.

'It's a sensible job you have up north, isn't it?' he asked at last, and she nodded.

'Yes.'

'And do you have a sensible boyfriend?'

She flushed at that. 'I do, as a matter of fact.'

'Is that who you're running from?'

'I'm not running.'

'I can pick running from a mile off.'

'You were running,' she said softly, 'when I first met you.'

'Well, you stopped that.' There was a moment's pause and then he added, 'Maybe I can stop you running.'

'Now, what do you mean by that?' she said, with more asperity than she'd intended. She lifted the bandages and started wrapping the leg again. She was thoroughly unnerved and it took real concentration to keep her hands steady and not jolt the leg.

'I could very much use a partner here in Birrini.'

'What—another family doctor?'

'The place is screaming for two doctors. Times like tonight. To not have an anaesthetist...'

'I live in Queensland,' she said flatly, trying to suppress a quiver of sheer panic running through her. Work here? With this man?

'But you don't want to be in Queensland.'

'I do.' She fastened off the bandage and rose. She should go. This conversation was far too intimate. Far too...threatening?

But she had to ask.

'Why are you in Birrini?' It had her fascinated. This man was a surgeon and a good one.
Why was he stuck in such a remote spot?

'I love Birrini.'

'Why?'

'My father was a fisherman,' he told her. 'I
spent my life here, by the sea.'

She nodded. It fitted. He looked weathered,
she thought. The look of the sea was in his eyes.

'Yet you did surgery,' she said, thinking it
through. 'Surely if you were intending to come
home to practise, you would have done family
medicine—become a generalist rather than spe-
cialising.'

'I didn't want to come home.'

'Why not?'

She should let him sleep. The bedside lamp
was all the light there was in the house. He was
deeply relaxed, lying back on his pillows, and
she knew suddenly there was never going to be
a better time to question this man. To find out
what made him run.

'All the time I was a kid here...' he said, and
his voice was almost dreamlike. He was drifting
to sleep and his voice was slurred. But still he
kept on. 'I wanted to see the world. I thought
Birrini was so narrow. My parents were really
happy here, but I almost despised them. There

had to be a great big wonderful world out there, so as soon as I graduated from high school I was out of here and I never looked back.'

'What happened?' she asked. She was almost unable to breathe. This night—this time—was weirdly personal. She felt as if she was probing into places she had no business being. But she couldn't stop.

'I was such a success,' he said wearily. 'High-powered city surgeon. Fantastic. I came down here every few months. To visit. To show off.'

'Oh, Harry, I'm sure—'

'Don't stop me,' he told her.

'I don't want to upset you.'

'It's not you doing the upsetting.' He fell silent for so long that she thought he was sleeping, but as she moved to turn away his hand reached out and grasped her wrist.

'I was engaged,' he told her. 'To Melanie. Before Emily.'

'I knew that,' she whispered. 'Lillian said she was killed.'

'She was. We came down for the weekend.' His voice was suddenly dragged down with exhaustion, but she sensed it wasn't his leg that was making him tired. This was some bone-deep weariness that had been with him for years.

'Melanie was driving her new toy—an open-topped roadster. All the horsepower in the world. Melanie was another surgeon, and money was the least of our problems. And Melanie...she was...well, Melanie was really something. Smart, ambitious, beautiful. I thought I was so in love.'

'You weren't?'

He shrugged. 'Love? What the hell would I know about love? I was stupid. We were stupid. Anyway, she was so proud of her new car. And my dad...he was always so kind. So kind. He asked her to take him for a ride in it. My dad, who didn't know one end of a car from another and couldn't care less about them. So Melanie took him out on the coast road. You've seen the bends. She was showing off. City doctor showing the country hick what it's all about. They went off the road about a mile from town and hit the rocks twenty metres below.'

'Oh, Harry...'

'Melanie died instantly,' he said, and his weariness was palpable. Bleak and unforgiving. 'My father had massive internal injuries. Maybe if we'd had another doctor here...maybe... But there was only me. There were no facilities. I couldn't operate on my own and he died being transported to Melbourne.'

He was still grasping her wrist. Lizzie stared down at their linked hands and slowly she sank down onto the chair she'd just risen from and took his hand in both of hers.

'So you decided to be sensible.'

'Of course I did.' His eyes were closed but his free hand came up to stroke the back of hers. So there was a linking of four hands. She needed it. She needed every vestige of warmth she could get.

'My mother was still here. Of course. I couldn't leave her. I came back here and applied to open the hospital. It had been shut for years because they couldn't get a doctor. I settled down and worked my butt off.'

'And your mother?'

'She died last year. She never got over my father's death.'

'And neither did you?'

'No.' There it was, in all its bleakness. The truth.

'So where does that leave Emily?'

'Emily?'

'Your fiancée,' Lizzie said gently, and Harry flinched. She felt it in his hands. She saw it in his face.

'I think I've been stupid,' he told her. 'Again. For different reasons but still stupid. Six bridesmaids.'

'It's a lot of bridesmaids,' she agreed, and received the first trace of a smile in return.

'A veritable horde.'

'Scary.'

'Very scary.'

She smiled. Enough. All she wanted to do for now—for some reason she couldn't figure out even to herself—was to stay sitting here. Holding this man's hand. Lighting the bleakness of his night.

But she had things to do. She needed to check on Lillian. She needed to…needed to…

She needed to leave.

'You ought to sleep,' she told him, and slowly, reluctantly she extricated her fingers from his. She rose and stood looking down at him. 'Do you want anything for the pain?'

'I don't have pain.'

'I'm sure you do.'

He smiled again, that wry self-deprecating smile she was coming to know. 'I'm fine, thank you, Dr Darling.'

The way he said it… The softness in his voice…

It was really, really stupid to find tears welling behind her eyes. Ridiculous.

And it was even more stupid to do what she did next. To lean over and let her lips just brush his.

The gentlest goodnight kiss.

It was not what most doctors did to their patients.

It was right, though. It was meant to be. It was…

It was very, very scary. She stood looking down at him in the half-light and she felt her world shift on its axis. She didn't have a clue what was going on here, but she knew that nothing could ever be the same again.

Emily. Edward. Queensland. Phoebe. Life…

The expression in his eyes was as confused as hers was. He couldn't leave, though. He was stuck in his bed.

It was up to her to break their gaze. To walk out of that room and close the door behind her.

And she'd never done anything so hard in her life.

'Phoebe?'

The big dog was sprawled full length over the kitchen floor, her nose pressed hard against her supper dish. She hadn't been fed for years, her expression said, and Lizzie managed a smile as she knelt and gave her great fat dog a hug.

'So you're pregnant. You must have been in love,' she whispered. 'What would you do?'

And then she thought about what she'd said. In love?

'That's one crazy thing to think,' she told herself. 'You've known him for how long?'

Ridiculous.

'How long did you know the father of your puppies?' she asked Phoebe, and Phoebe looked soulfully up at her and then looked again at her supper dish.

'Right. Think of practicalities. Men are no use at all, unless you want kids, right?'

Phoebe nudged her supper dish again.

'Right.'

She should ring Edward.

Why on earth?

'To ground myself. To remind myself that this is a tiny part of my life and as soon as Harry McKay gets himself married I'm out of here.

'You could leave now.

'What, and leave him like this?' It was a ridiculous conversation, and Phoebe wasn't the least bit interested. She'd figured that Lizzie's attention wasn't where it should be and was gazing at her dish now as if it was the last bastion of hope for the entire canine race. Hopelessness personified. Starvation was just around the corner. The end of the world was nigh.

'Oh, for heaven's sake...'

Lizzie gave herself a shaky laugh, hugged her dog again and rose to her feet.

'The vet said no. You've had enough tonight. You've had more than enough.'

Phoebe looked up at her, her great ears almost lifting with effort. Hope, her eyes said. Death had been looming but now the kitchen cupboard was opening. A sliver of light was appearing in the darkness of desperation.

And Lizzie couldn't help herself. She smiled. 'OK. Half a cup. No more. I'll buy your love with half a cup of dog food and then I'll forget love altogether.'

Phoebe looked at her as if she was out of her mind.

'Until suppertime tomorrow,' Lizzie corrected herself. 'Fine. I have the devotion of a dog and I'd better look after it. Because that's all I'm going to get.'

Memo:
I will not scratch my leg. Scratching is an entirely inappropriate response to stimuli of damaged nerve endings.

I will not think of Lizzie. Of the way her fingers felt. Of the way her lips brushed mine.

I will not scratch my leg.

I'll just rub my fingers really gently...

I will not think about Lizzie.

I will not... I will not...

I will forget about inappropriate responses. What a man's got to do, a man's got to do.

And a man has to scratch!

CHAPTER SIX

HARRY was still sleeping when Lizzie was ready for the day.

Lizzie ate her breakfast at dawn, gave Phoebe a snack, showered and readied herself for work—she'd dressed Corporate this morning, in the neat little suit she'd been wearing when she'd crashed into Harry—and then opened his bedroom door.

He was out for the count.

He'd been awake during the night. She looked at the bedside table where she'd left a glass of water and four painkillers. Two of the tablets were missing.

Good. He might have played a hero in front of her, but he had enough sense not to suffer unnecessarily.

His body needed sleep.

He looked good asleep, she thought, her eyes softening as they rested on him. He'd thrown back his covers—the room was heated and the back-slab and bandages would be hot. He was bare-chested, his hair was tousled from sleep and his face on the pillows looked unlined and younger than his thirty-odd years.

He'd had a bad time, she thought ruefully. To lose a fiancée…

Actually, maybe he'd lost two fiancées. Where was Emily?

What was the line? To lose one husband is careless. To lose two is just plain ridiculous.

She smiled but the laughter didn't reach her eyes. There was so much about this man that she didn't understand.

Or maybe she did. He was being sensible. He'd had one crack at being the big city specialist, and it had been a disaster. It had hurt everyone around him. So for now he wouldn't follow his heart. He'd follow his head.

He'd marry Emily despite her six bridesmaids.

What a waste.

She should leave him to sleep. She had no business staring at him. Any minute he'd wake and question her motives, and she hadn't the faintest clue what her motives were.

She'd just stand there for one moment longer.

Memo:
I will not open my eyes.
I am asleep.

Maybe I'll open my eyes and think of something clever to say. Something flippant.
I will not open my eyes.

Being a country doctor was really strange. The medicine Lizzie was accustomed to was trauma in a big city hospital. Here she was, at Birrini Elementary School—practising *medicine*?

There was no trauma in sight—but there was definitely need. The needs of Amy—the little girl who'd been so badly bullied—and Lillian's needs. Lillian, whose self-confidence had to be built at all costs.

'So tell me again what you want me to do?' Lillian was asking, and Lizzie had to collect her breath for a moment and think about it. What *was* she doing here?

Lizzie and Lillian—and Phoebe—were backstage at the junior school hall. Out the front were fifty-odd pupils, all lined up and waiting for the results of Lizzie's art competition. Somewhere among them was Amy, a little girl who'd had to nerve herself to come to school this morning. A little girl whose home life was almost as awful as school.

And Lizzie's idea to use Lillian to help fix it... Would it work? Lillian was shaking like a leaf.

Maybe it wasn't such a good idea, Lizzie thought, but, then, it had been partly Lillian's own plan, put forward with such tentative anxiety that to knock it back would have been unthinkable. And it had just seemed to fit so well. Two pieces of a puzzle coming together. Or two damaged kids helping to heal each other.

'You're the best artist in Birrini,' she told Lillian stoutly, pushing away any qualms that she might yet have a disaster on her hands. 'You won the state competition last year and May tells me that every kid in town was so jealous they could spit.'

'They're never jealous of me.'

'You know they are,' Lizzie told her, fleetingly touching the girl's face. 'Or course they are. You're beautiful, you're clever and you're talented.'

'I'm not.'

'You have a father who tells you you're not,' Lizzie said bluntly. 'That's because he can't see what's so obvious to everyone else. You have a brother and a sister who are academically brilliant. One's doing medicine and one's doing law. That's their thing. Your thing's art.'

'Art's useless.' The burgeoning confidence of the girl back in the hospital had all but disappeared. To appear in public... Her terror was palpable.

Lizzie sighed. Should she let Lillian off the hook? Do the presenting herself?

No. It'd reinforce all the negatives that Lillian had instilled in herself. They had originally been a product of her father's belittling, but they were now self-feeding.

'Are you going to tell Amy that art's useless?' she demanded. 'You know what's happening to her. We've agreed—and it was partly your idea—that winning here will be a chance for her to break this horrid cycle of self-doubt. The same self-doubt you're coping with. I thought you agreed you'd do this for me.'

'I did.'

'You can do this, Lillian. You know you can.'

'I want to be sick.'

'If you're sick now, then Amy keeps on being bullied. Is that what you want?'

'N-no.'

'Then let's do it.' Lizzie stooped and hugged Phoebe, her grin belying how sick she felt herself. Would this work? Please...

*   *   *

Harry found May taking obs and waylaid her. He was feeling so disoriented it was crazy. He'd stayed in bed for as long as he could bear it but this was ridiculous. This was his hospital. His patients. What was Lizzie doing taking over as if she belonged?

'Where is she?'

'Who?' May turned from her patient and smiled. She knew darned well who he was talking about.

'Lizzie.' He corrected himself and gave a rueful smile to old Mavis Scotter in the bed. 'I mean Dr Darling.'

'She's taken Phoebe and Lillian down to the school.'

'Phoebe and Lillian?'

'Yep. Girl and dog. Both of them.'

It was nine in the morning. May had only had eight hours off duty and she was, in reality, too weary to be working.

One of the town's bank of semi-retired nurses would take her shift if she asked. Maybe she should—but, heck, she was enjoying herself here.

There were, in fact, other reasons May needed to work. Reasons May didn't want to think about.

But meanwhile... Dr McKay had hobbled into the ward looking angry. Which was really interesting. There was no need for the man to be angry, she thought, but anger was definitely there.

May was more and more interested. And so was old Mavis. As would half the town if they could see the expression on Harry's face.

'Phoebe and Lillian,' she agreed, and watched his face change. Nurse and patient grew even more interested.

'Why?'

'It's the announcement of the winner of the art prize.'

'Amy's art prize.'

'We don't know that, Dr McKay. Anyone could win.' May pursed her lips and tried to look prim—and failed.

'You're telling me it's not rigged?'

'The most deserving child will win, and that's all I'm saying.'

'So Lillian's watching Lizzie present a rigged prize.'

'Lillian's presenting the prize.'

'You're kidding.'

'Nope.' She gazed at him 'Aren't you still supposed to be in a wheelchair, Dr McKay?'

'I not only shouldn't be in a wheelchair,' he said grimly, 'I shouldn't be here. Call Jim. I want him to drive me down to the school. Lillian's going to present the prize? We could really use this. If she'd told me... If I have time... Quick, May, ring Jim now.'

'Yes, Doctor.' And she smiled to herself as she made her way to the nurses' station. Very interesting indeed...

Phoebe the basset could play a crowd better than anyone—or anything—that Lizzie had ever seen.

The great fat basset, beautifully adorned in a purple bow that was wider than her ears, waddled out to centre stage and beamed at the audience with all the charisma of a comedian who'd been treading the boards for fifty years.

The school children were seated in rows facing the stage—fifty or sixty children ranging from six to twelve. It was a really scary audience, Lizzie thought as she followed Phoebe onstage and thought again, What have I done? This was such a far cry from the emergency room she was accustomed to. She was sticking in her oar and she suddenly wasn't the least bit sure it was going to work.

It had seemed such a good idea at the time.

Beside her was Lillian, and the tension ema-
nating from the girl was real and dreadful. But
at least she looked great, Lizzie thought. She
herself had opted for clinical—her neat little suit
with a stethoscope just peeping from her top
pocket to emphasise the fact that she was who
she said she was. But Lillian... They'd stopped
by her home and chosen jeans, a clingy little top
that hid her almost skeletal frame but made her
look really cute, and a gorgeous tie-dyed purple
scarf to tie back her blonde curls and make her
look almost bohemian. She was your absolute
picture of an artist starving in the garret, Lizzie
thought appreciatively, and she knew, looking
down at the sea of little girls looking up at her,
that they'd all think Lillian looked lovely.

Would it be enough?

But it was time for her to speak. The principal
had introduced them and it was Lizzie's turn.

These kids had decorated her—Harry's—
apartment. She owed them.

Was this really medicine?

It was country medicine, she knew. This was
good. If it worked.

Please...

'I'd like to thank you all for my wonderful
paintings,' she told them, and thought, How can
I be so nervous in front of kids? But she was.

Her knees were shaking. 'I love every single one of them and if I were judge they'd all win. But Phoebe's only willing to relinquish one of her puppies to the winner.'

Phoebe's beam grew broader at that. Honestly, you'd swear the crazy basset knew she was the star attraction.

'So here's Lillian,' Lizzie managed. 'Here's Lillian, who everyone tells me is Birrini's best artist and is headed for fame and fortune, to announce the lucky winner.'

Applause.

And, as if on cue, Phoebe stood up and strolled to the edge of the stage and wagged her tail. Which was just as well as it gave Lillian breathing time. She looked petrified.

'I did it without falling over,' Lizzie breathed as she propelled her forward. 'So can you.'

'You were scared?'

'Petrified.'

'O-OK.' Lillian seemed to take heart from shared terror. She took a deep breath and turned to the audience. And spoke. While Lizzie had trouble breathing.

But Lillian had it under control. Describing the paintings in glowing terms. Sounding just like a professional.

'I looked for great texture,' she told them. 'Wonderful composition and balance. I looked for potential. As Dr Darling has said, though, there can only be one winner.'

She's doing it, Lizzie thought, stunned. The girl seemed to be gaining in stature while she spoke. She knew her art. In the few days Lizzie had known her it was the one area where she lit up. How dared her father belittle this? This gift.

To lose a life like this to anorexia would be such a waste.

And then she looked up from the stage and caught sight of a cluster of people at the back of the hall.

Harry.

It wasn't just Harry. There were also Lillian's parents and Amy's parents. How had he collected them at such short notice? she wondered, bemused. There was also a small group of boys in their late teens in the uniform of the senior school. Big boys. Good-looking kids, toting guitars and a drum kit.

The whole group had Lizzie intrigued, but mostly Lizzie just looked at Harry.

He was propped up on crutches, leaning against the wall, surveying her with a look that was half a smile, half a question.

She couldn't look at Harry now. She needed to focus all her attention on Lillian. This was such a gamble.

'And the winner is…'

Lillian paused for effect. Phoebe turned to her and pointed her wet nose in the direction of the envelope. Lillian tore open the envelope.

'The winner is Amy Dunstan.'

Silence.

Would it work?

There were a few groans as various hopefuls realised they hadn't won. There was a collective regroup. And then as the diminutive Amy got to her feet, unbelieving, bewildered, the school community burst into clapping. If they couldn't win, at least one of their own was going to obtain one of these wonderful puppies.

Amy still looked bewildered. She'd been shadowed by her brother's death for so long she'd stopped believing good things could happen. A tiny child for her age, wearing glasses that were too thick for her elfin face and clothes that didn't quite fit, she looked almost bereft.

But not for long. A smiling Miss Morrison came forward and took her hand, leading her up onto the stage. The little girl looked as if her knees were about to buckle under her, but her face was breaking into the beginnings of a tremulous smile.

'I...I've won?'

Lillian looked at Lizzie to confirm Amy's win, but Lizzie shook her head and stepped back. This was Lillian's call.

'You've won,' Lillian said gamely. And then added, with even more confidence, 'It's a wonderful picture. You should be very proud.' She held out her hand and Amy took it, and Lizzie almost crowed in delight. Two damaged kids, helping each other to heal. They had a long way to go. But maybe...

'I've won a puppy?' Amy quavered, and Lillian didn't even look at Lizzie this time.

'You have,' she said. 'If you want one.'

If she wanted one. Amy stared down at Phoebe, and Phoebe, rising majestically to the occasion for such a dopey mutt, sauntered over to Amy and stuck her nose straight up Amy's sweater. Amy was so short and Phoebe was so...elongated that the basset's nose came straight out of the neck of Amy's sweater. Amy gave a little giggle of pure pleasure and wrapped her arms around Phoebe.

If ever there was a case of kid needing dog, this was it.

But… Amy's jumbled emotions were letting in an awful thought. 'Mum won't let me keep it,' Amy whispered, the beginnings of joy fading almost as soon as they'd appeared. 'Mum says she couldn't bear a puppy. Scott wanted a puppy. Before…before…'

The principal spoke up then, a stern-looking lady in her sixties. 'I think you'll find your parents approve of the idea,' she told Amy. She looked down the hall for confirmation, to where Mr and Mrs Dunstan were standing beside Harry.

Lizzie hadn't thought of involving them. She'd asked their permission—of course—but to bring them here…

It had been a masterstroke. Mr and Mrs Dunstan were staring up at their daughter as if they hadn't seen her for years and, even from the stage, Lizzie could see the beginnings of tears on Amy's mother's face. And for the first time since Scott had died, she suspected, these tears weren't for her son.

'Of course you can have a puppy,' the woman called in a choked voice. 'And if anything happens to Phoebe's puppies, we'll get you another.'

Something happen to Phoebe's puppies? The thought was almost unthinkable.

Everyone was looking at Phoebe now. Horrified at the thought. But prenatal nerves were obviously for pansies. Not for bassets. Phoebe wriggled free of Amy's sweater and waved her tail like a windscreen wiper. Something happen to her puppies? No way!

Great.

But they hadn't counted on Amy's detractors. There were a couple of kids who really had it in for Amy, Miss Morrison had told Lizzie. They were the school toughs and they were here. The two tough little girls were sitting at the end of one of the front rows, and as the proceedings had unfolded they'd been watching with increasing displeasure.

Now, as Phoebe stared out into the audience in dopey confusion, one of them found her voice.

'Yeah, so she gets one of the puppies. So what? No one else would want them. That dog's really, really stupid.'

'She's not.' Amy gasped back her dismay. Lizzie moved to the child's side and noticed with approval that Lillian did the same on the other side.

This much at least was good. Lillian was seeing Amy's plight more clearly than her own at the moment. It was medication for Lillian all on its own.

But not for Amy. Lizzie had set this up wanting the entire school to be jealous of Amy's puppy—of the prospect of the puppy, and then the puppy when it eventuated. This was far better than just handing an eight-week-old pup to the child. But the prospect of a pup... No, it'd extend the anticipation. Extend the pleasure. Extend the sensation of Amy being the luckiest kid in the school instead of the unluckiest.

And here were these two horrible children trying their best to undermine it.

Maybe she should go back to emergency medicine, Lizzie thought ruefully. That's what she was good at.

The principal was opening her mouth to speak, about to attempt to undo the damage. Could she?

She didn't have to.

'If anyone else wants a puppy, I'm afraid they need to join a queue,' Harry called, and Lizzie whirled to face him.

What?

'They've been bespoken as band mascots,' Harry said, limping forward on his crutches so he had the whole audience in his sights. He grinned, that wide lazy grin that had her heart almost stopping within her. 'They're going to be groupies. Basset groupies.'

This was crazy. The entire population of Birrini Elementary School was staring, fascinated, as Lizzie and Harry conducted a conversation over their heads.

Lizzie was so far out of her depth here that she felt she was drowning. She didn't get involved. She never got involved!

She was standing on a school stage with an emotionally damaged eight-year-old clutching one hand and an anorexic teenager clutching her sleeve. Her great fat dog was sitting on her feet, the whole school was watching...

And what had Harry said? Basset groupies?

Harry was motioning to the boys at the back of the hall, who were grinning self-consciously back at him. 'As everyone here knows except you, Dr Darling, these boys are the Birrini Punk Squirrels.'

'The Birrini Punk Squirrels...'

'They look pretty ordinary in their school clothes,' Harry called. He was grinning like a Cheshire cat, thoroughly enjoying himself. 'But you should see them in leathers.'

'Or bare-chested,' one of the boys yelled, and the kids in the hall dropped their collective jaws to their ankles.

'I know them,' Lillian breathed in Lizzie's ear. 'They're the best band. The best. They get gigs all over the state…'

'They're adopting your pups,' Harry called. 'Until such time as they go to nice family homes, Phoebe's puppies will be the band mascots. The boys want a pup apiece.'

'But—'

'The boys don't mind if Amy has one puppy,' Harry called. 'But the rest are taken. Now…if the principal's agreeable… We're celebrating a few things here. No one's made a public announcement about Lillian's brilliant art win and it needs to be celebrated. Amy's done a fantastic painting, too, and there's a puppy coming her way. And the boys want to celebrate the impending birth of Phoebe's pups. In honour of all of that—do you mind if the boys take centre stage, Mrs Hill?'

'Go right ahead.' The principal looked even more out of her depth than Lizzie. Which was clearly impossible. 'Go right ahead, Dr McKay,' she repeated weakly.

'Fantastic.'

So the stunned group on stage stood to one side and the four boys surged forward with whoops of delight and enthusiasm, bringing their guitars and drums along with them. They hauled out their shirts, loosened their school ties, fixed their young audience with grins that only eighteen-year-old boys knew how to produce—and proceeded to transfix every single member of the audience.

'You realise they can't have the puppies.'

They were in Lizzie's car, heading back to the hospital. Phoebe was sound asleep in the back, worn out by all the excitement.

Lillian was being taken back to the hospital via a coffee-shop—'Because maybe we need to talk,' Lillian's mother had said, fixing Lillian's father with a look that said if he knew what was good for him he'd shut up about doctors and lawyers and start saying good things about artists.

Amy had been soundly hugged by both her parents, assured they really meant what they'd said about keeping a puppy and was now surrounded by a group of envious little girls who really, really wanted to be her friend.

The Punk Squirrels were walking back to the senior school, probably taking the longest route they could think of.

'Of course they can't keep them,' Harry agreed. 'That'd be counter-productive. I can't really see those lads being saddled with the responsibility of puppies for many a year yet.'

'But you said—'

'I said the puppies would be the boys' mascots until they were ready to be family pets. That means the puppies can be mascots for about eight weeks. Being mascots doesn't necessarily mean they have to travel with the band. Maybe a small silver basset shape to hang from their navel piercings will do the trick.'

'I don't believe this,' Lizzie said faintly. 'How on earth did you manage it?'

'I thought this was a great idea,' he said, looking sideways at her in the car. 'When May told me what you intended I just extrapolated your theme.'

'Extrapolated...'

'Expanded.'

'I know what extrapolated means.'

'That's good,' he said approvingly. 'Very good.'

'Don't patronise me!'

'I would never patronise you,' he told her, and all of a sudden the laughter wasn't there. Nowhere. Not even close.

'But...' Her voice was a squeak and she tried desperately to turn it into a cough, and tried again. 'But...'

'I know those kids that have been bullying Amy,' he told her, taking pity on her discomposure. 'That's what being a family doctor is all about. You get to know your patients, warts and all. The kids that have been doing the bullying... Kylie and Rose come from dysfunctional families. They've had rotten treatment in the past. I have Social Services involved now, and I'm hoping it's not too late. They've grown into two little thugs. Giving Amy a puppy by having her win the art competition was a brilliant idea but those two are going to try and take her glory.'

'So...'

'So the boys—the Punk Squirrels—are in year twelve at the senior school. They're considered so cool by the rest of the town kids—and by themselves—that they're practically ice. And they owe me.'

'They owe you?'

'The four of them came down with mumps, one after the other,' Harry said, grinning. 'Just before last year's State Bandfest. The whole town was riding on the outcome and if it had got out that the boys couldn't play because of mumps they'd have been laughing stocks.'

'So...'

'So they contracted epidemic parotitis.'

'But…' Lizzie frowned. 'Parotitis is mumps.'

'Oh, come on, now.' Harry was grinning at her across the car. 'How can you say such a thing? Mumps is an undignified kid's complaint, engendering fat necks and not a lot of sympathy. Parotitis, on the other hand—whew. An almost unheard-of infection that maybe has something to do with parrots. Weird and exotic and just the thing for a bunch of cool eighteen-year-olds with navel piercings.'

'You're kidding?'

'Nope.'

'And you got away with it?'

'We got away with it, yes.'

'And they recovered?' Lizzie was choking back laughter. The man was clearly brilliant.

'They did,' he told her. 'In the end half the kids in the town came down with a really un-dignified case of mumps, so their audience would have been halved. But still they stood out as being different. The boys' parents were in the know, but no one else. While we were immu-nising kids for mumps as fast as we could go, we also had parents enquiring about immuni-sation for this strange new disease called paro-titis. But we were able to explain that it was only kids who were really weird who got par-

otitis, and not the general run-of-the-mill population. The band's street cred soared.'

'So today...'

Harry's grin deepened. 'So today was pay-
back time. They've made a fuss of Phoebe, the
thought of weird basset-something puppies as
temporary mascots appealed enormously, and as
a byproduct they've also seen what Lillian did.'

His grin faded, to be replaced by a look of
intense satisfaction. 'You've done good there,
too, Dr Darling. For Lillian to do that...
Incredible.'

'It was you who did good,' Lizzie retorted,
trying not to flush. 'Getting her parents there.'

'They were due for a kick in the butt. When
May told me what was happening I rang them
and said their kid was doing them proud so to
get to the school and make a fuss of her. They'll
bring her back to hospital—we have a long way
to go with her yet—but we're making progress.
You're making progress. More progress than I
would have dreamed possible.'

'It feels good,' Lizzie said, and he nodded.

'It does. Do you want to stay?'

'Stay?'

'Stay here. I've told you. I could really use a
partner. Birrini is big enough to employ two

doctors full time, and to have a sympathetic female doctor...'

'I don't do family medicine.' Her fingers were suddenly tightly clenched on the steering-wheel and Harry glanced across at her, his face thoughtful.

'You do, you know,' he told her. 'You care.'

'It's because I care that I can't do it.'

'It's because I care that I'm forced to do it,' he said, and his voice sounded strained suddenly, all traces of laughter gone. He sounded suddenly bereft. 'Alone.'

Lizzie thought about that as they swung into the hospital parking lot. They came to a halt but made no move to get out of the car. Instead, she stayed silent, staring out the window at the little hospital nestled in the trees. A county bush nursing hospital. It was about as far from her ideal medical environment as she could imagine. And here was this man...

'Alone, you said,' she murmured cautiously, and Harry nodded.

'Alone.' The desolation was still in place.

She ventured a fast glance at him and then looked away. He looked miserable.

She thought about it. About the way he'd said the word. *Alone*...

And she cast him another sideways glance. To confirm her suspicions.

'Phoebe does this,' she told him. 'About half an hour before dinner.'

He looked startled. 'Pardon?'

'She looks devastated. As if the end of the world is nigh and the only person who can save her from starvation or worse is me.'

'You're telling me...'

'It's your cocker spaniel look,' she explained apologetically. 'If you hadn't said *alone* with quite that amount of pathos...'

'Hey!'

'You need to work on your act, Dr McKay. It's good but not good enough. I've been trained by an expert. After Phoebe...no, a mere *alone* doesn't cut it. You're OK to hop into the hospital alone, then, Dr McKay?'

'Yes, but—'

'Fine, then.' She grinned. 'See you later. Come on, Phoebe, we have work to do.'

Then, as he broke into stunned laughter, she climbed out of the car and slammed the door behind her, clicked her dog to heel—sort of— and then walked into the hospital, leaving him staring dumbfounded after her.

'He's sweet on you.'

Two hours later Lizzie just happened to be

walking past Lillian's door. The girl had been dropped back at the hospital by her parents and had gone instantly and soundly to sleep. With a body as severely malnourished as hers was, it took little to exhaust her. Now, though, the minute Lizzie walked through the door she pushed herself upright in bed and giggled.

'The guys say he's nutty.'

'The guys…' Lizzie said blankly. She looked down at the girl in the bed and couldn't refrain from a feeling of accomplishment. OK, she didn't get involved—as a rule—but this morning she had and it seemed to have worked out just fine.

'The Punk Squirrels. They walked back to school past the coffee-shop Mum and Dad had taken me to, and Dad called them in and bought them Coke and cake.'

'Your dad?' Lizzie asked, amazed, and was rewarded by another giggle.

'I know. It's amazing. You know my dad's an accountant? He's so big on professionalism. My sister and brother…Mardy's a doctor and Stephen's a law student and he's crushed that I'm never going to be any good at those things. And he condemns everyone who doesn't want what he wants. But Mum and I went to the girls'

room and Mum said Dr McKay came around
this morning and gave him the rounds of the
kitchen table. He said if the world was full of
doctors and lawyers and accountants it'd be a
really boring place and I had a skill that most
doctors would kill for and he said I had to follow my heart…'

'He said that?'

'He did. He said following rules rather than
following your heart leads to despair and that's
where I am—though I don't know about that—
but Mum hugged me and cried and said she's
proud of me and so's Dad. I wouldn't have
thought it, but then when we came out of the
bathroom Dad was talking to the guys. I mean
really talking to them. Asking about their songs
and their production. Like he was really interested. And then he started being really helpful
about the way they did their distribution over
the internet and they talked for about half an
hour until Mum noticed I was nearly asleep and
that the boys should be back at school. Then she
hauled Dad off to pay the bill—but it was an
excuse, I reckon, 'cos she left me with the guys
for about ten minutes and they told me then that
Dr McKay had been real funny and he'd insisted
they had to help you.'

'Me?'

'They said he couldn't keep his eyes off you on the stage. And Mum said when he was talking about following his heart…well, she was sure he was talking about Emily. Or not talking about Emily, if you see what I mean.'

'Hmm.' Lizzie was trying hard to take this all in but it was too hard. Too…close? In times of stress—revert to medicine. 'I don't think I do see what you mean.' She tried a smile. 'It sounds really complicated. Local knowledge needed.'

'Yeah, but you know…'

She didn't know anything, and this had to stop. Right now! 'What have you had to eat?' she demanded, and Lillian grinned.

'You're changing the subject.'

'You're absolutely right I'm changing the subject. I'm a doctor, aren't I? And Dr McKay's love life is strictly Dr McKay's business.'

'If you're sure…'

'What have you had to eat?'

Lillian gave her a long look and then shrugged. Moving on. For now. 'I ate a cake at the coffee-shop,' she told her. Then, as Lizzie fixed her with a look of disbelief, she amended it. 'OK. Half a cake. But it was a really big cake and I did try. Mum was watching me and she didn't say a word—that's Dr McKay telling her not to nag—but I could tell she was pleased. And then I ate half a round of sandwiches when I got back here and Dr McKay sat with me until I went to sleep so I swear it stayed down.' She flushed a little and then looked anxious. 'Lizzie...I mean, Dr Darling...'

'Lizzie's fine,' Lizzie told her. She wasn't staying here. She wasn't feeling like a doctor. The treatment they were using on Lillian was unconventional so maybe formalities weren't required. And she could see that more confidences were about to be delivered.

But Lillian had changed her mind. 'It doesn't matter.'

'If it affects the way you're feeling then it matters.'

Lillian hesitated.

'Lizzie,' she said, and Lizzie pushed away the white coat image and stethoscope and she smiled.

'Lizzie. Definitely Lizzie.'

And somehow it worked. Lillian's defences crumpled still more. 'Joey...the skinny one in the band...' she started, obviously searching for courage as she went. 'He said after I get out of here, can he take me to the pictures? What...what do you think?'

Lizzie raised her eyebrows and tried not to smile. Tried not to shout! 'Joey, hey? The drummer. Hmm. Maybe the question shouldn't be, what do I think? Maybe it should be, what do you think?'

'I think...maybe he feels sorry for me?'

'Do you think someone like Joey would ask you to the pictures if he felt sorry for you?'

'N-no.'

'Then maybe he thinks you're cute,' Lizzie said, and stooped to give the girl a kiss on the forehead. More unprofessionalism but, hey, she was getting used to it. 'As I do. Cute and artistic and kind to small children and ill—but recovering fast. How about that for a prognosis?'

'I guess...it's a good prognosis.'

'It's a fine prognosis,' Lizzie told her. 'Let's keep working on it. Joey, hey? Well, well, well.'

'Dr McKay, hey?' Lillian mimicked, snuggling down under the bedclothes and smiling shyly up at her. And then past her. 'Well, well, well.'

'Dr McKay?'

She hadn't heard Harry. He'd come up behind her so suddenly that when he touched her arm she nearly jumped out of her skin.

She whirled and he was sitting innocently enough in his wheelchair, his leg out before him.

'What do you think you're doing?' she spluttered before she could collect herself, and he gave her a lopsided smile that had her even more flustered.

'I'm tired of being on crutches. I'm practising my wheelchair skills like a good little patient.'

'If you were a good patient you'd be in bed.'

'No.' He smiled across at Lillian. 'Exercise in moderation. I'm sure that's right. You don't have to be in bed to be a patient. Miss Mark, what are you doing in bed at this hour of the afternoon? You're looking far too healthy to be in bed.'

It was a lie. Lillian had been in hospital for three weeks now and the child still looked skeletal. Her kidney function was compromised, her liver function worrying. They had a long way to go. But this morning they'd seen what could be possible.

It was hard, though. She needed to be in some specially run facility where there could be supervision as needed, but also lots of things to keep the hyperactivity associated with anorexia satisfied. But, failing that, Lillian had to stay here. At home she couldn't be supervised, she'd find laxatives or buy them, she'd purge...

She was making the first moves toward a cure, but long term there was so much to do.

Meanwhile... Lizzie looked down at Harry and she could almost see his sharp mind focusing on Lillian's needs. Keeping the girl happy. If Lillian became bored out of her mind, there was no way they could keep her here. This wasn't a locked psychiatric ward.

'You're bored,' he said, and Lillian nodded.

'You're right. I shouldn't be in bed.'

'What do you want to do?'

'Get out. Do some exercise.' She looked wistfully at Harry's wheelchair. 'Those things look fun.'

'They are fun,' Harry said promptly. 'I'm getting better and better. Want a demonstration?'

'No,' both girls said together, and he winced.

'Ouch. A man has some pride...' Then he looked more closely at Lillian's wistful face. 'It is fun,' he said slowly. 'But it'd be much more fun if I had someone to show off to. Hey. I know what. Can I offer you an excursion in one of the hospital wheelchairs?'

Lizzie blinked. Whatever she'd expected, it wasn't this.

But Harry, once fixed on an idea, was unstoppable. 'The corridor is empty. There's not a decrepit patient in sight. Everyone's cosily settled for their afternoon nap except you, Lillian, and your two friendly physicians. And I'm sure our Dr Darling will turn a blind eye to some high jinks.'

'High jinks,' Lizzie said feebly. 'High jinks? What is this? Gidget Does Birrini?'

She was ignored. 'How about we do some wheelies?' Harry was teasing, and by the sideways glance he cast at Lizzie it wasn't just Lillian he was teasing. 'We could really burn some rubber here if you're willing.'

'Do wheelchairs go that fast?' Lillian demanded, her eyes sparkling, but Lizzie was shaking her head in disgust.

'Dr McKay, how do you think,' Lizzie asked carefully, 'that you got that broken leg in the first place?'

'You hit me,' Harry said blandly, and she choked.

'You got it being a total twit.'

'I did.' He looked crestfallen. 'You're right, of course. So I did. Thanks for reminding me. And speaking of reminding... Dr Darling, I think Phoebe's pining. She needs an antenatal check. Off you go and do some doctoring. Lilly, are you ready?'

'Really?' Lillian was tossing her bedclothes aside, her face a picture of disbelief warring with hope.

'Outside,' Lizzie said helplessly, trying not to laugh. This wasn't like any hospital she'd ever been in. 'You're not burning rubber in any hospital corridor I'm a doctor in.'

'Fair enough.' Harry appeared to think about it. 'How about into town and back again, then, Lilly?'

'No!' Lizzie was definite and once again he appeared offended.

'Hey, you're no fun,' he complained. 'Go do your antenatal checks, Dr Darling. Let me and Lilly figure this out.'

'You'll fall out and have to go back to Melbourne to get your leg reset,' Lizzie managed, and he grimaced.

'I won't fall out. And, besides, it'd make you stay a bit longer. We'd like that, wouldn't we, Lilly?'

'I'm staying till the pups are born. No longer.'

'We'll see,' he said enigmatically. 'Lilly, what about a race out on the path down to the sea?'

'Why there?' the girl said, but she was already hauling on jeans over her pyjamas and was reaching for socks and shoes.

'It's a mossy path. If we fall out then Dr Darling won't get to patch us up.'

'I wouldn't anyway,' Lizzie muttered, and they both smiled. She stared at both of them—and then threw up her hands in disbelief. 'Fine, then. Kill yourselves. See if I care.'

'So you'll watch?' Harry was smiling.

'Certainly I'll watch.'

'You're sure we can't use the road into town? If we don't go on asphalt our wheels will get stuck.'

'Great. You're not built for speed.'

'Who says?'

'Me,' she said, and put her hands on her hips and glared.

Standoff. They glared at each other while Lillian watched, fascinated.

'If we use the garden path, will you referee?' he asked at last, and she groaned.

'You're never serious.'

'I'm serious.'

'Lilly…'

'It's all right, Dr Darling, I won't hit him,' Lillian told her seriously. 'I won't knock him over.'

'You'll never let him win?'

'Do I look like a girl who'd let a man win?'

'Yay for you.' She'd protested enough. 'Fine. OK, Lilly, if you agree to win then I agree to act as umpire. And if either of you breaks another leg, I wash my hands of the pair of you.'

'After you set our legs?'

'Before. I swear it. And then I'll patch your legs without morphine!'

CHAPTER SEVEN

Memo:
I will not break another leg.
I will not think about Dr Lizzie Darling watching me every step of the way.
I will not think about how much more fun life is—how much more alive I feel—and why...

THEY raced an hour later, and by the time they started the entire hospital was out to watch.

Certain rules had been decided. Once Lizzie agreed to take part she decided she was there to enjoy herself.

Lillian was given the wheelchair built for speed. Harry was removed from his slick little set of wheels and put in the hospital's spare chair, which looked more like a bath chair than a wheelchair.

'It was built for pushing elderly dowagers around fashionable watering spots last century,' Harry complained, and Lizzie raised her eyebrows in gentle mockery.

'We have two wheelchairs. Do you want Lillian to have this one?'

'Yes,' he said, and there was general laughter.

And Lillian… It had been a great day for her. She'd been put into hospital because she'd been starting to show signs of kidney failure. Her weight loss was making her cachectic. So she needed to stay. She needed medical supervision. But her problems weren't purely physical. The long-term answer to anorexia wasn't to be found by keeping her huddled in a hospital bed, though, with the stresses of the real world ready to crowd in on her the moment she was released.

So…maybe it was a good thing that she was here, Lizzie conceded, in this tiny community hospital where the boundaries between in and out were so blurred.

They had all the patients lined up to see, plus every staff member. There were also a few visitors. In particular, one very interesting visitor.

There was Joey—the drummer—out of his school uniform now. He'd just happened to be wandering through. He'd expected to visit a girl in a hospital bed, Lizzie thought, and she watched in satisfaction as he tried really hard to look cool and disinterested. How much better that he see this glowing, laughing kid lining up at the start of a wheelchair race and raring to go.

'Your brakes are still on, Lillian,' Lizzie called, and it was Joey who ducked forward and fiddled with the lever.

'Hey, that was my only advantage,' Harry complained. 'You weren't supposed to tell her that.'

'She'd beat you even with the brakes on,' Joey said stoutly. And then, because he was standing right beside her and suddenly his cool disinterest didn't seem as important any more, he bent and gave Lillian a swift kiss on the lips.

It was her first kiss. The whole audience could see. She stared up at Joey in amazement and her face flushed with colour.

'That's for luck,' Joey said softly.

Lizzie thought, What have we done?

But Lillian was growing more flushed by the moment. They needed to get the attention off her.

Harry sensed it almost as Lizzie did and he had the perfect solution.

'What about me?' he demanded, affronted. 'Don't I get a kiss for good luck?'

'Not from me,' Joey said, and grinned.

Whew! This felt great, Lizzie thought. Great. She dug her hands into the pockets of her white coat and thought, I'm working. I'm on duty as a doctor and here I am out in the sun with a whole bunch of people whose laughter is a medicine all by itself.

'Dr Darling, you need to do that,' Lillian retorted, and Lizzie hauled herself back to attention.

'What?'

'Give Dr McKay a kiss for good luck.'

'I'm the referee. I'm meant to be impartial.'

'It's the referee's job to make sure both contestants start on equal terms,' Harry told her. 'You've given me a turn-of-the-century bath chair and now you're refusing to give me a good luck kiss.'

They were all watching her. The oldies were especially delighted—they'd toddled out *en masse* from the nursing-home section of the hospital and their faces were all alight with interest.

Go jump, she should tell them. This man is engaged to Emily.

But that would be making too much of it. This wasn't the time to be talking of engagements or weddings. It was purely a good luck kiss and it meant nothing at all. If she didn't... If she didn't, then they could well ask why not and...

And she'd waited too long already. The silence was growing loaded.

Right. One good luck kiss coming up. She stepped up to Harry's chair and bent and her lips lightly brushed his forehead...

No.

That was not his intention. Before she could guess what he was about he'd caught her, reaching up, and taken her face between his broad hands and directed her kiss.

To his mouth.

And this wasn't some feather-light kiss of good luck. This was a kiss! While the entire population of Birrini Bush Nursing Hospital cheered and applauded, Harry McKay kissed his doctor-cum-partner.

And his doctor-cum-partner's senses shuttered down right there and then.

She managed a gasp—sort of—but then her brain decided it had other things to concentrate on that were much more important than gasping. There was the vague sound of clapping and cheering, but it was only vague and then it disappeared entirely. There was just Harry.

He was pulling her down to him, his lovely hands were through her hair, holding her close. His mouth was on hers. In hers. The feel of his mouth... It was the only reality there was.

She felt herself sinking…sinking… He was tugging her in closer; warmth and desire were flooding her body from the toes up… And then he slipped his tongue into her mouth. She was bending to meet his kiss—the man was in a wheelchair, for heaven's sake—but she wasn't aware. She was only aware of the taste of him. The feel of him. Her knees were giving way. Dear heaven, was she going to sink to the ground while the entire population of Birrini Bush Nursing Hospital looked on?

They wouldn't mind. The cheering and laughter were gaining momentum so that even she could hear them.

She didn't care. She couldn't care. She grabbed at his arms for support and her eyes closed, and he was all there was.

Here was her heart. All there was in her world was the heat of his mouth, the feel of his fingers running through her hair and the sensation that all that had ever been wrong in her world was suddenly right.

She was where she belonged. She was home.

'Do you think we should run the race without them?' It was Lillian, choking back laughter. Joey was behind her and his eyes were sparkling with mischief. 'Should someone ring Emily and tell her the wedding's off, then?'

Emily.

The word was enough to haul them back. To have them pulling away from each other. To have Lizzie step back, confused and disoriented, her hand flying to her lips, reluctant to lose the sensation of such sweet pressure.

Emily. The race. Medicine. Edward. Queensland.

Jim, the hospital orderly, had been standing to one side, holding Phoebe by the collar. The big dog seemed to have been adopted by the entire hospital, and wherever there was action there was Phoebe. Now, sensing Lizzie needed something to ground her—anything—Jim released her collar and the basset nuzzled her way forward and pushed against her mistress with a whine.

It helped. The dog's flabby warmth against her legs gave her back reality. It enabled her to say with a voice that was almost steady, 'Now, are you still saying you've been disadvantaged, Dr McKay? If you want a longer good luck kiss than that, you'll have to ask Phoebe.'

It broke the tension. Almost. There were faces in the crowd that stayed speculative, but it gave them the footing to pretend that the kiss had been a joke.

As it had been, Lizzie told herself desperately. It couldn't mean anything. Could it?

'It's time to race,' she told them. 'Anyone want a good luck kiss from the dog or shall I start you off?'

'Let's go,' Harry told her, and the look he gave her was strange. There was laughter there—teasing—but there was also something…something more.

Something she didn't want to think about.

'On the count of three,' she said breathlessly. 'Beat him, Lilly. Show him what a woman can do. One, two, three… Go!'

Lilly beat Harry. Of course she beat him. Some things were never in doubt.

The path was wide and strewn with leaves, weaving in and out of the big gums overshadowing the gardens leading down to the headland. The first part was cultivated garden but outside the hospital boundary it became a rougher track, flattened by locals exercising their dogs or kids putting their trail bikes through their paces.

Lilly was a wraith-like figure but with the anorexic's typical compulsion for exercise she was a fighting fit wraith.

Harry was super-fit.

Lilly's chair was streamlined and light. Harry's was big and cumbersome, but it was more stable, meaning that he didn't have to slow as much over the worst of the bumps.

For Lizzie, following behind, she could almost see the moment when Harry backed off—not much. He surged ahead a few times as if desperately trying to maintain the lead. But enough…

They reached the point where the headland gave way to sand dunes and then to beach. Jim had dashed ahead, Phoebe waddling beside him, to set up flags.

Lilly hit the flags a nose ahead and the cheers could well have been heard in Tasmania.

'You didn't let me win,' Lilly demanded as, flush faced and triumphant, she turned to face her opponent.

Harry gasped for breath, took a couple of seconds to answer and then told her, 'Of course…' gasp. 'Of course I let you win. It was sheer good manners on my part.' Gasp. Gasp. 'I'm the world's kindest doctor.'

And Lillian's face relaxed into a wreath of smiles. 'You didn't,' she announced with jubilation. 'I beat you.'

'Thanks very much,' Harry said morosely, and then, as Phoebe waddled up to Lillian, wagging her tail, he groaned.

'That's right. A kiss for the winner.' Then he looked around for Lizzie. 'Hey…'

'Don't even think about it,' she told him. 'Winner takes all.' And she walked over and gave Lillian a kiss that wasn't anything like the one she would have liked to have given Harry.

He was a wonderful doctor, she thought. This community was so lucky to have him. He was so caring. So giving…

Emily was lucky to have him.

And that was a stupid thought. Stay uninvolved, she told herself severely. Stay out of the hearts and minds of this community. Of Harry.

He's getting married and you're moving on.

'I'm going back to the hospital,' she told him. 'Some of us have work to do, even if others can afford to spend their time in idle wheelchair racing.'

'All your patients are here,' Harry pointed out.

'I'll find some who aren't.'

'Lizzie?'

'Yes?' She met his eyes. The community was crowding around now—there were people be-

tween them—but somehow their eyes locked
and held.

'Thank you,' he said simply, and she knew
he was talking about much more than refereeing
the race. 'Thank you, Lizzie.'

'I'm just glad you didn't break your leg.'

'Me, too.'

It was still…more. They were grinning at
each other like fools. It was ridiculous, Lizzie
thought desperately. What she was feeling was
really, really ridiculous.

But she couldn't help what she was feeling.

'Are you still on duty?'

Lizzie had run a shortened version of the evening clinic—or not so short as everyone was
talking about the race and everyone wanted to
quiz her about the kiss—and by the time she
returned to the hospital it was almost eight. She
found May carefully changing the dressing on
old Mrs Scotter's leg. Mavis Scotter had cut it
a week ago—chopping wood, of all things—and
by the time she'd come to see Lizzie it had been
an infected mess. The old lady's skin was so
parchment-thin that they'd be lucky if it healed
without a skin graft, but they were doing
their best.

The dressing had to be changed. But May shouldn't be doing it.

'Am I imagining things or have you been on duty for over twelve hours—plus, you had barely eight hours off last night?'

'You're imagining things,' May told her, and Lizzie looked more closely at the normally cheerful nurse.

'May?'

'Yes?' May smiled brightly at Mrs Scotter. 'The leg's going really well, Mavis. And did you hear about our Dr Darling kissing Dr McKay?'

'Stop changing the subject,' Lizzie told her, but the nurse kept on.

'Where's Dr McKay now?' May asked.

'Phoebe-sitting, I hope. And resting his leg. Which is what you should be doing.'

'What?'

'Resting.'

'I need to—'

'I'll finish Mavis's leg.' Lizzie smiled at the old lady. 'That's OK, isn't it?'

'Oh, yes, dear.'

'I'll do it,' May said, but Lizzie wasn't listening.

'There are other nurses available to relieve you.' Refusing to take no for an answer, Lizzie lifted the crêpe from May's hands and started winding. 'I've seen the roster. Emily leaving hasn't made us that short-handed.'

'No, but…'

'But what?'

'I'd kind of like the overtime,' May confessed. 'And I'm not tired. I'm really not.'

Lizzie looked at her. Really looked at her. Not tired? Ha! There were shadows under her eyes and the normally effervescent nurse looked strained to breaking point.

Why hadn't she noticed that?

There was an easy answer to that. She'd been caught up in her own emotional turmoil.

But it wasn't the time to press for reasons now. Not with Mavis hanging on every word and her wound still half-dressed.

'Ring one of the relieving nurses,' she told May gently. 'Do it now. I'll finish here. Go home.'

'But—'

'Or go and sit in the nurses' station and put your feet up until I get there,' she told her. 'But you're officially off duty. I'm taking over. Go.'

At least it was something to talk about. Something she needed to talk about, rather than facing this tension that was between them.

Lizzie finished the dressing, went out to discover a relief nurse already on duty and May gone, and went through to the doctor's quarters to find Harry cooking steak and chips.

'If you were any longer I'd have shared the steak with Phoebe instead of you,' he told her. He was back on crutches—or rather he was using one crutch and one leg while he stood supervising the steak. And he had his frilly apron on again, which for some stupid reason had the capacity to make her want to melt into a puddle of sheer, stupid desire.

How could she want a man who wore a frilly pink apron?

How could she not want him? She wanted him with a fierceness that was threatening to overpower her!

Boy, should she take a cold shower.

Instead, she talked about May. Somehow.

'She carries a load and a half,' Harry told her, nicely deflected as she helped him carry his steak and chips to the table. 'She thinks the world of her Tom, but he has a weakness for gambling. He got himself into a real mess a couple of years back. I arranged for him to go to counselling in Melbourne—he did a full residential course to try and kick the habit and he's pretty much controlled, but he's confessed to me that he's struggling. If May's looking grim then my guess is that that's what it'll be. She'll have just received a bank statement. I'll go out and talk to him tomorrow.'

Lizzie ate a few chips and thought about it. 'Um…what business is it of yours?' she asked at last.

'He's my patient.'

'But this is gambling. Not medicine.'

'You don't think that gambling is a medical problem?'

'I don't see much of it in the emergency department where I work,' she admitted. 'I'd have thought it was more to do with Social Services or family counselling.'

'There's no Social Services counselling available in Birrini—and even if there was, Tom wouldn't go. Not in the first instance. Not without my intervention.'

'So you take it on board…'

'I don't have a choice,' he said gently. 'If Tom becomes obsessed with gambling again…well, you're telling me May's looking exhausted already. She starts taking on more shifts to make things pay. Her health suffers. She works long hours and the kids suffer. Tom gets more and more isolated. I've seen suicides as a result of problem gambling and that is very much my business.'

'But—'

'Medicine's not just bodies,' he told her. He was watching her, his eyes strangely questioning. Challenging. 'It's about the whole person. The whole family. I'm a family doctor, Lizzie. I believe I'm a good one. I didn't want to come here but now I'm here I wouldn't swap it for anywhere else. And…' He paused as if thinking about it but then obviously decided to go ahead anyway. 'I believe you'd make a fine family doctor, too,' he told her. 'If you could find the courage.'

'The courage…'

'You'd like to work here,' he said gently. 'You had one disaster—'

'And that's where I'm stopping.'

'Stay here,' he told her. 'There's no stopping. You're a family doctor and you know you are.'

Silence. She'd started eating her steak, but now she laid her knife and fork down. And looked across the table at him.

He looked straight back at her, his eyes calm and steady.

'You kissed me,' she said, and his gaze didn't waver.

'That's got nothing to do with this.'

Like hell it didn't. 'I see.' She bit her lip. 'So you're offering a professional partnership here.'

'Of course I am.'

'There's no "of course" about it,' she snapped, and speared a chip with her fork so savagely it went flying off the plate and landed on Phoebe's nose. Phoebe looked stunned. She surveyed the chip from all angles, decided that to refuse it would be denying the gods, ate it with care and then put her nose skywards in the hope of another gift from heaven.

'See what you've made me do?' Lizzie demanded, furious. 'Phoebe's a pregnant mum and she's on a pregnant mum diet.'

'Hey, you fed her the chip.'

'You made me.'

'Oh, yeah, right.'

This was a ridiculous conversation. She refused to continue. She went back to demolishing her chips with a ferocity born of anger. One after another. Eat and get out of here...

'It's only a job,' he said at last, and got a king-sized glare for his pains.

'So why did you kiss me?'

'If I remember rightly, it was you who kissed me.'

'You know very well that it was you...' She faltered at that. No. He didn't know very well it had been him. It had been both of them. What she'd felt had been a coming-together of a man and a woman that had packed a lethal punch. She'd never felt anything like that. Not even with Edward.

Edward. Now, there was a steadying thought. Edward was enough to steady anyone, she thought miserably, and he was a good note to end this conversation on.

'I can't stay here,' she told Harry, standing up and taking her half finished plate to the sink. Phoebe's tail started rotating like a miniature— or maybe not so miniature—helicopter. 'Forget it, kid,' she told the dog. 'You need vitamins. Not fat.'

'Why can't you stay here?' Harry looked interested—no more—and the urge to throw the plate of leftovers right at his unfeeling head was almost overwhelming. 'Because you kissed me?'

'You kissed me. And no!'

'Then why?'

'Because I'm engaged to be married,' she told him. 'Just like you. You have your Emily right here in Birrini and I have my Edward. In Queensland. As soon as Phoebe's pups are born, that's where I'm heading. Where I belong. Now, if you'll excuse me, I have things to do.'

There was a long silence. Her words had changed things. The silence was almost over-whelming.

But why had her words changed things? she thought sadly. All she'd done had been to put things on an equal footing. Harry was engaged. So was she. He could take it and lump it. At least it gave her some pride. At least it let her meet his gaze and tilt her chin and not feel as if she was melting...

Who was she kidding? She was definitely melting.

Maybe he could see it. His eyes were spec-ulative. His eyes saw too much for their own good.

'The hospital's quiet,' he said at last. 'There's no work. What do you have to do?'

'Lots of things.'

'Like?'

This was crazy. She'd had enough. 'I need to go into my bedroom and watch my toenails grow,' she snapped. 'Anything. But I'm not staying here with you a moment longer than I need to.'

CHAPTER EIGHT

Memo:
I have no business even questioning Lizzie's engagement. I have no business even thinking of it.
I have no business thinking about her kiss. Her body. The way she curved into me…
I have no business thinking of anyone.
Maybe I can stay single for ever. Memo to me: Get a life. Alone.

IT WAS an interminable two weeks.

Given any other circumstances, Lizzie could have enjoyed herself enormously. She loved this little hospital. The locals had adopted her as their own. They pampered her already pampered pooch. They brought her gifts. They showed in every way they could that she was entirely welcome, and that Harry's suggestion that she should stay wasn't his plan alone. Everyone in the town thought it was a great idea.

She should tell everyone that she was engaged to Edward, she thought. She'd been surprised that Harry had kept it to himself. But he'd never mentioned it. He'd never asked her why she didn't wear a ring. Even when the phone went late at night and it was obviously Edward, he made no comment. He'd hand the phone to her, his face expressionless, and find some reason to leave the room.

She should tell him…

She should tell Edward…

Tell them what? She didn't know. All she knew was that she was increasingly confused. All Harry had to do was walk into the room and her confusion levels rose to fever pitch, where she couldn't think logically at all.

She loved this place.

She loved…Harry?

Nonsense. That was nonsense. Emily was out there house-hunting or doing whatever women did when their wedding was delayed, but soon she'd be back and the bridesmaids would take their place and Harry would be married.

So she had no business even thinking of Harry like that.

So instead she tried her best to concentrate on the other parts of Birrini life that she was growing to love. Which was easy enough as Birrini was wrapping itself around her heart, insidious in its sweetness.

Lillian was growing healthier by the minute. She still hated to eat—that was going to take months to cure. She still couldn't be trusted not to bring the food straight up again. It had become such a habit now that the sensation of a full stomach was completely alien to her.

But Harry had her working now—gently, though, and not with the frenetic over-activity she'd been building up to for the last couple of years. Every morning she'd do schoolwork set by her teachers, and in the afternoons either her mother or one of a roster of hospital volunteers drove her to the local kindergarten where she gave art lessons.

Harry's suggestion to work at the kindergarten had been met with joy. The only stipulation was that if she needed to go to the bathroom, someone had to bring her back to the hospital. To be accompanied by a nurse. She hated the stipulation, but she was starting to accept her condition enough not to rail against it.

And her art lessons were fantastic. She put her heart and her soul into them. For two hours every afternoon she forgot all about her stomach or her looks or food. She simply was. Even her father was grudgingly beginning to concede that maybe Harry's and Lizzie's combined treatment was starting to work. Maybe he could be proud of his kid if she turned into an art teacher.

And every evening Joey wandered past, and the two heads bent over the lesson plans she had for her littlies the next day.

It was deeply satisfying—country medicine at its best.

And Amy… The little girl who'd been a cowering mess two weeks ago was practically transformed. Every afternoon after school a gaggle of little girls with Amy at their centre arrived to visit Lizzie's great basset.

'When are the puppies due?' Lizzie was asked over and over, and the vet was consulted as well. The dates on the calendar were being ticked off and never had babies been more anticipated.

Amy was radiant.

Whenever she saw her, Lizzie looked at her with pleasure, and then she caught Harry looking at her looking at Amy—and tried hard to school her face into some sort of dispassionate doctor-patient assessment.

It didn't work. She loved what was happening here and she couldn't disguise it.

It didn't make one whit of difference, though. She had to leave. She had to move on.

'So have these babies and we'll get out of here,' she told Phoebe, and the big dog heaved her pregnant self into a position where she could nuzzle her mistress's nose. Lizzie hugged her and thought, At least I have Phoebe.

There was no sign of Emily.

'She's taken leave,' Harry said shortly when she ventured to ask, and Lizzie knew better than to push further. May might have helped—May was never backward about asking questions—but May was still preoccupied, shadowed and worried.

'I've pushed May's husband but I'm still worried,' Harry admitted during one of those moments that Lizzie worked so hard to prevent. Times when they were alone. But this one had been unavoidable. Lizzie, on instructions from the orthopaedic surgeons, was removing the staples from his wound and preparing to put a fibreglass cast on his leg.

It felt so strange. Wrong. Too intimate for words. There was no way she could keep professional detachment here. Since that first night when she'd rubbed his leg she'd had one of the nurses do it for her. It seemed too intensely personal. It seemed too intensely personal now—to be working on his leg while he lay on the bed and looked up at her—but there was no way they could avoid it. To send him to Melbourne to get a cast fitted was ridiculous when she had all the skills.

'You've pushed Tom?' She was concentrating—really hard—on the staples. They were lifting cleanly away, dropping with a clink, clink, clink into the kidney dish under her hand.

'He says he's not gambling,' Harry told her, and she could tell by the tension in his voice that he was finding this situation as difficult as she was. But he was focusing on Tom. There was no choice.

'Most problem gamblers deny it.'

'I believe him.'

Lizzie nodded. She removed the last of the staples. 'This is looking really good, Harry. Your surgeon's done a great job. You'll hardly have a scar.'

'I don't mind a scar,' he growled. 'I wouldn't have a leg if it wasn't for you.'

'You wouldn't have run into me in the first place.'

'No. I might have run into a ruddy great truck going like a bat out of hell. I might have been a squashed puddle in the middle of the road instead of a workable doctor with a scar in the middle of my leg.'

'So you're grateful to me?' Her eyes flashed laughter and to her amazement she found he was smiling back. His smile never ceased to amaze her. What his smile did to her...

'You don't know how much,' he told her.

Which sent her straight back to the defence of silence.

Where was Emily? Lizzie knew she phoned occasionally—occasionally she'd heard Harry take a short, terse call—but there seemed little other contact. Anyone would think he didn't want to get married, she thought. A good doctor—a family doctor—would press the point.

She wasn't Harry's family doctor. She was caring for his leg and if she let herself care for any other part of him then she was in major trouble.

Tom. Concentrate on Tom.

'So if Tom's not gambling, what's wrong with May?'

'Tom doesn't know. He's worried about her, too. She's not sleeping and she keeps taking on more and more shifts when she doesn't need to. I've put a stop to it—told her five shifts a week maximum—but then I find she's taken on a bit of private nursing. Old Ern Porteous should be in the nursing home but he won't go. The district nurse calls on him twice a day but he really needs more than that. His family's paying May to spend two hours there after each shift.'

'She's raising three small boys. She'll kill herself.'

'Yeah. But she won't admit to me that anything's wrong. Or to Tom.'

'Nor to me,' Lizzie admitted. 'So what do we do?'

'We can't force the truth from her,' Harry told her. 'If Tom really is gambling... They're both proud people.'

'But if they're self-destructing...'

'We're only doctors,' Harry said heavily. 'There's only so much we can do. The rest is up to them.'

'It hurts,' Lizzie said slowly, and he nodded.

'You really are a family doctor,' he told her. 'You care and you care and you care. Just like me. Now all that has to happen is for you admit it.'

'Right.' She stared down at his leg. The swelling had subsided enough for him to wear a cast and, considering the way he refused to submit to being an invalid, the sooner he had a protective cast on it the better.

'Lie back down,' she told him. He'd propped himself up so that he could see and the sensation of his face being so close to hers was unnerving.

'You want me to go back to being a patient—instead of a person?'

'Of course I do.'

'Because you can cope with the world that way.'

'I can cope with you that way,' she muttered, reaching for the wrapping to use under the fibreglass. 'It's the only way it's going to happen. So get used to it.'

Life became more complicated after that. With a plaster boot fitted to his new cast, there was no stopping Harry. Wherever Lizzie went he seemed to be there. He still used a crutch, but he was so subtle she couldn't hear him coming.

The place was too small for two doctors, she thought—but then had to concede that it wasn't. It worked brilliantly with two doctors. It was only that one doctor stiffened and couldn't keep her mind on her work any time the other doctor was present.

'When did you say Phoebe's due?' He asked her that at breakfast the day after she'd fitted his new cast and she sighed. Phoebe's confinement was starting to be all she thought of herself. He obviously wanted to be shot of her and she felt the same about him. They had to get distance. They must!

'Soon,' she snapped. 'The vet says any day. When's Emily due home?'

'Soon. Any day.'

'Great.'

'But you can't leave until the puppies are eight weeks old.'

'Which gives you time to have your wedding and honeymoon.' Under her breath she added, 'And keep yourself out of my way.'

'Right.'

'Fine.'

It was ridiculous. Two grown doctors who re-acted to each other as if they were impregnated with some electrostatic charge. Harry just had to walk into the room and her skin tingled and she had to concentrate so hard…

'I don't know where that girl's gone,' Mrs Scotter muttered as Lizzie changed the dressings on her leg again. Mavis was home from hospital and Lizzie had taken to dropping in on the old lady every morning. Her leg was finally starting to heal, but Mavis valued Lizzie's visits more than the healing.

As Lizzie valued Mavis. She'd miss her when she left.

She'd miss so darn much.

Um…maybe she needed to concentrate on Mrs Scotter. What had she asked? 'What girl?' she asked.

'Emily.'

Emily. The absent fiancée. Right.

'She's shopping for things for her house.'

'She's been gone for weeks. She's never been gone for that long. If it was my fella who'd broken his leg the day before the wedding and I knew that he was sharing a house with a woman like you, well, I'd be a damned fool for staying away that long.'

'Maybe she knows she can trust Dr McKay,' Lizzie said stiffly. 'Your leg's looking great, Mavis. Who's chopping your wood now?'

'I am. Who do you think? Do you think she should trust Dr McKay?' The old lady's eyes were boring into her, and Lizzie flushed and rose.

'I have no idea. I hardly know the man.'

'You've shared a house with him for weeks.'

'We hardly see each other.'

'More fool you.'

'Mavis, where's your woodshed?' Lizzie demanded. Enough was enough.

'Out the back. Why?'

'Because I intend to chop you some wood. I need to vent some frustration and chopping wood seems an ideal way to do it.'

He found her there, half an hour later. Harry limped around the side of the house following voices and the sound of the axe, and he stopped dead at the sight of her.

It was harder than she'd anticipated. Mavis had given her a splitter—an axe specifically designed for splitting logs—but she'd discovered it was science as well as muscle. So Mavis was standing back out of range while Lizzie chopped.

She had a pile now that was starting to give her satisfaction, but maybe it was only enough for one or two nights' fires and she needed to do more. Her face was flushed bright red. She was exhausted, but she knew that if she stopped Mavis would take over. And some things were unbearable.

Some things other than Mavis's lack of wood...

'What do you think you're doing?'

Her axe landed with a thud and the log of wood spilt into two very satisfactory halves. A splinter flew backwards and caught her on the leg and she winced. Drat.

And here was Harry marching toward her, barely letting his crutches touch the ground.

'Are you out of your mind?'

'Nope.' She barely looked at him. The tension between them was nigh on intolerable.

'What do you think you're doing?'

'I'm being a family doctor,' she said through gritted teeth. 'I'm engaging in a bit of preventative medicine.'

'Preventing what?'

'Mavis killing herself.'

'So you're chopping with bare legs.' He pointed down. She'd worn her standard little skirt out on house calls. Nice shoes. City shoes. Or they had been nice city shoes three weeks ago. They'd seen a lot of life since then. 'You'll kill yourself instead.'

'I'm fine.'

'You're not fine. If Mavis's eyes weren't going she'd have told you what I'm telling you now,' he told her. He stepped forward and took the axe from her hands. 'You're likely to get hit in the leg by splinters. You already have been hit on the leg by splinters. You're bleeding.'

She looked down at a trickle of blood coming from a scratch on her knee.

'Not very much.'

'I suppose you think this is what doctors do.'

'You're telling me you wouldn't chop wood.'

'I can chop wood. I choose not to. I concentrate on my areas of expertise. As you should. As you especially should. If I was a damned fool city kid, I'd give axes a wide berth.'

'Hey.' She glared. A damned fool city kid? Who did he think he was talking to? 'Give me my axe back and go back to your crutches.'

'Mavis…' He sidelined her nicely, turning to the old lady who was watching with avid interest. The tension between the town's two doctors hadn't gone unnoticed by Mavis—or by anyone else in town. After the kiss on the day of the race there had been talk of little else. That and Emily's continued absence…

'Mavis, I'll ring the local Rotary club and have someone come out and chop you enough wood to last for the rest of winter,' he told her, and Mavis grinned, a gap-toothed smile that contained more than a hint of mischief.

'It's more fun watching you two fight over it.'

'Maybe, but I'm on crutches and she'll kill herself.'

'She—the cat's mother?' Lizzie asked, dangerously polite, but she was ignored.

'I'll take her back to the hospital.'

'Would you mind not talking about me as if I'm an inanimate object?'

'Would you mind acting as if you had a brain in that frothy head of yours?'

'Just because I'm trying to be a family doctor...'

'You can't be a family doctor unless you commit. And you're not committing.'

'Hey, who's talking about not committing? You're the one who crashed into my car rather than get married.'

All of a sudden things were way, way too personal. Mavis's grin had faded. But her ears were positively flapping.

'This is not...' Harry took a deep breath. 'This is not the time.'

'Is there ever a time?'

'No.'

And then his mobile phone rang.

It was just as well, Lizzie thought, trying to regain a semblance of her dignity. Things had moved far, far too fast. If Phoebe hadn't been so loaded down with puppies she'd have done what she should have done three weeks ago. Gone back to Queensland.

To Edward?

Maybe.

But then she stopped thinking about herself. She was hauled out of her emotional turmoil. Harry had replaced the cellphone on his belt and his face told her that what he'd heard was suddenly deathly serious.

'We need to go,' he told her. 'Sorry, Mavis. There's been a car crash. May's driven her car off the road near her home and crashed into a tree. The car's hanging over the cliff and she's trapped inside.'

The police car was already there. Two more cars. A school bus. Blocking the road.

They'd driven in Lizzie's little car, hurtling along the back road with more daring than sense. But...

This was May, Lizzie thought over and over again, and by the look on Harry's face he was feeling exactly the same. And when they pulled up...

The road here twisted around the cliff face. The car looked as if it had veered off the road, smashed into a tree and swung around, so the back half of the car was hanging over a ten-foot drop down to the beach below.

No!

They were out of the car, hauling the emergency equipment Lizzie had started carrying as normal, running past the school bus where a frightened teacher was yelling at his charges to stay sitting, to not move, that everything was OK.

Stupid thing to say. Everything wasn't OK.

The local police officer looked up as they arrived, his face sagging in relief. 'Doc... Thank God...' He had a fire extinguisher playing on a stream of petrol oozing from the still steaming car. There were two men—the drivers of the other two cars, presumably—sitting on the bonnet of the crashed car and Lizzie saw with horror exactly why. The whole car was threatening to slip.

And the car...

The old Ford was crumpled beyond belief, its back wheels hanging out over the edge and still slowly spinning. It looked a complete wreck. A disaster prepared to topple into the sea and be forgotten.

Except...through the shattered glass they could see May, folded forward on the steering-wheel, her hair sprawled out over the dashboard and her hands reaching out...

As Lizzie stared in horror she stirred and lifted her head. She stared out sightlessly and let out a slow keening moan of horror.

There was blood on her face. Blood on her hands...

'I'll go in,' Harry snapped. 'Car's not stable.'

'And neither are you,' Lizzie told him. 'You can't manoeuvre yourself in that space with one good leg. I'm going.' May was trying to move now, struggling feebly against whatever was holding her. She couldn't shift. The keening increased.

She couldn't bear it. 'May...'

'We need chocks. We need weight on the hood to keep it stable.' Harry looked around as a tow truck screamed up beside the school bus. 'Thank God. Someone, get that bus turned around. Get the kids out of here. Hell, Les, May's kids are on that bus.'

'I'll do it,' someone said. People seemed to be arriving from nowhere. 'And I'll take the kids home to the missus.'

'We need chocks,' Harry was yelling. 'Now. We have to get this thing stable.'

'I'm lighter than anyone. We can't leave her. If she tries to haul herself out she'll cut herself to ribbons.'

'But—'

'I'm going in,' Lizzie said. She grabbed a pair of protective gloves from her bag and hauled them on.

There was glass and torn metal everywhere. She was wearing a miniskirt…

'Take my overalls,' the police officer volunteered. He'd been wearing some sort of protective all-in-one suit over his uniform but was already hauling it off. She wasn't objecting. She grabbed it and pulled it on. It was ten sizes too big but it was better than nothing. Way better than nothing.

But Harry was still aghast. 'Lizzie, no…'

'There's no choice. Get those chocks in place and don't let me fall,' she told Harry, and she didn't wait for him to answer. The overalls clipped into place. She was secure as she was going to be and May needed her.

She didn't try the driver's door. The roof and the driver's side were appallingly crushed. The passenger door was almost intact and was one of the few parts of the car which were almost on the road. But inside…

Thank God for the overalls. That and the gloves saved her from the worst of the mess. Because it was a mess. The roof was crumpled. There was blood, bare metal and glass all over the place and she could hardly move without cutting herself.

Her gloves weren't thick enough.

Outside people were yelling. She could hear Harry, his voice tight with desperation. 'Get those damned chocks. Someone…I need the bag from the back of our car. The fluid bags. Everything.'

There were people shouting. She couldn't hear…

And May was thrashing about, yelling, and quite literally trying to crawl out the window.

'May, no.' Lizzie caught her hand and held on, gripping hard. Forcing her to be still. Sort of. 'May, I'm here. May, you must be still.'

The car was rocking. Dear God, the car was rocking.

She couldn't think of that now.

This was like some ghastly nightmare. The sight of May—*May!*—covered in gore. The smell of it. The sharp edges—glass everywhere. May!

She had to fight with that. She had to stay impartial. She was trying desperately to help, but May was beyond working with her. She wanted out. She was desperate to get out, flailing, moaning…

Out of control.

At least she was making a noise, yelling now. That was a good sign—the only good sign. She was alive and she was conscious and her airways were obviously clear. And she was at least aware enough to know that she didn't want to be there.

There were people sitting on the hood right in front of her. Stabilising it.

She blocked out the thought of what the car had looked like. How many men did it take to stop a car from toppling over the edge?

Harry was out there. He wouldn't let it fall.

The thought steadied her. He'd be in here if he could. So she had to work as expertly as he would.

The medical stuff. Training. Think, Lizzie, think.

Check the chest. Has she got good oxygenation? Are the airways clear?

Is the abdomen rigid?

Are there signs of a bleed or sensory loss? Is the blood pressure coming down? Were there changes in colour in the skin or the pupils? Those were all problems where she'd have to intervene hard. Cerebral trauma was an obvious worry, as was spinal damage…

Think! Assess!

Then Harry was there—just outside her door. Behind her. She couldn't see him but she could hear him.

'Cervical collar,' he said, and it was in her hand.

That was hard. May wouldn't keep still. 'May, you must…' But May was past hearing.

But finally she did it, working her way around the twisted metal and broken glass to get May into a cervical collar. Then some oxygen, and eventually she managed an intravenous line into May's arm for fluids and morphine. She took a quick blood pressure and pulse reading. The numbers weren't good. The BP was a low 90 and the heart rate a high 120.

Lizzie could see she'd taken a knock to the head. She was disoriented and there was a huge swelling under her right eye so she guessed she'd fractured a zygoma, the arch of her cheek-bone. There was a long, full-thickness laceration on the right side of her mouth and an ugly degloving injury had peeled back the skin on the back of her right hand.

She was worried about May's legs. The low BP was a possible indicator of an active bleed, but she couldn't see below her upper thigh. The legs could have been crushed.

That was why she couldn't move. The legs…

'Stay still.' Harry's voice was urgent. 'They're hauling the car back. Hold—'

'May, keep still!' Lizzie urged, and held onto her as the car lurched savagely sideways, up. And stilled.

'You're safe. The car's stable,' Harry told her, and she gave him a fast relieved smile that didn't quite come off.

What about the leg? If she could see…

Harry was almost in the car with her now, fitting a clear plastic soft protection sheet. They still couldn't come near to getting her out. The dashboard seemed to have almost folded completely around her.

'We're cutting,' Harry said. 'Get out and let me take your place.'

'Go find your own car wreck,' she tried. He didn't smile. But he didn't try and force her out either.

May was still moaning. Ten milligrams of morphine and still there was pain. There was a condition in medicine often referred to as the 'golden hour'. Lizzie knew of it and was afraid of it. It was the first sixty minutes or so when the body appeared to compensate for whatever had happened to it. Internal haemorrhage initially could be hidden as the survival mechanism kicked in. Heart rate and blood pressure could rise, adrenalin flowed and the victim would seem to be coping. But the bleeding inside could continue and the patient could crash. Hard.

There was a machine working outside—horrible. Resembling nothing as much as a great, silver-crabbed claw, its job was to chew away metal. Glass was spraying inwards and the sound was terrible. In the confined space every noise was magnified and Lizzie couldn't stop May's fear from escalating. 'Soon,' she told her. 'Soon. Harry will get us out.'

'Tom…'

'Tom and Harry will get us out,' Lizzie whispered. 'Our men.'

And then they did it. The rescue ram seemed to just bulldoze the dashboard away, and with the pressure gone May started to lift her legs.

'Immobilise first,' Harry was saying urgently, but May was having none of it.

'Tom. Tom. Tom,' she was crying over and over again as she tried again to haul herself free. Harry was on her other side now; together they were trying ever so gently to turn her.

'No!' She screamed against their struggles and her legs suddenly lifted.

Harry's eyes met Lizzie's, urgent, and she knew what he was asking. They had the equipment. In one swift movement Harry had the concave spinal board under May's rear, and thirty seconds later they had her out of the car and into the waiting van that served as the local ambulance.

Her leg was bleeding fiercely from a jagged gash. Harry had a pressure bandage on it almost as soon as it was visible.

But still May fought him, incomprehensible in her terror. 'More morphine,' Harry decreed.

And finally—finally—she relaxed and her eyes fluttered closed.

'Now we find the real damage,' Harry said grimly. 'Let's go.'

Three hours in surgery. Three hours of intense, silent work, while both of them came to terms with what had happened—and what had nearly happened.

Three hours while the world changed for both of them.

And when they were finished and had stepped back from the table, all pretence was stripped away. They knew what was between them. Now all they had to do was decide where to take it.

If they took it anywhere at all.

CHAPTER NINE

THEY went out to the waiting area where Tom was. Of course he was waiting. He was grey-faced and sick.

Harry had sent out news before, but one look at Tom told Lizzie that he hadn't believed the good news.

He had to believe it now, though she could scarcely believe it herself.

'Tom, she's going to make it.' Harry hauled off his theatre mask and knelt in front of Tom. The big man was ashen, his cheeks lined with tears. He'd been leaning over, his face in his hands, and Lizzie could see the pressure marks where he'd pushed hard.

'It's crazy. Crazy...' Tom looked up at Harry and his face said he still hardly believed them. 'You mean she really will live?'

'She's been lucky,' Harry said. 'A broken cheekbone, a couple of fingers that will take a while to heal, some nasty cuts to her hand that we've taken a long time to close...' He cast a sideways look at Lizzie that was almost a smile. 'Our Dr Darling is quite a needlewoman—I doubt a plastic surgeon could have done better. And May has a deep laceration to her leg. She's had a fair bang to the head but the X-rays are coming up OK.'

'I'll take her home…'

'In a few days. Yes.'

Silence. 'She thought I was gambling again,' Tom said heavily, and Harry nodded.

'She did. I came out and told you that. You told me to butt out of what wasn't my business.'

'I was bloody angry.'

'I know. If I remember rightly, you told me to go to hell.'

He groaned. 'I've been a fool.'

'Why?' Harry was still kneeling before the big man while Lizzie watched silently from the background. 'Tom, why? You know she's been busting a gut because she thought you were spending money again. She's taken on extra shifts. She's not been sleeping. Just like—'

'Just like when she had to.'

Silence. Harry had lifted Tom's big, farm-worn hands and was stroking them, as a father might have stroked a child. That was what Tom needed most desperately now, Lizzie thought. Warmth. And Harry could give it. He imparted warmth, spread it. He cared so much…

Not for her. Lizzie shivered and hugged herself. Shock had had time to take hold now. Emergency back in the city wasn't like this. Not when you knew the people. Not when you cared so much that your guts hurt...

'You mean she didn't have to?' Harry was asking, and Tom shook his head, his misery a tangible, awful thing.

'No.' The farmer looked up at Harry, a sudden surge of anger suffusing his face. 'Dammit, do you think I'd go back again? To gambling? I lost our house. I darn near lost May and the kids. I pulled myself out of the gambling habit just in time and it nearly killed all of us. So now...do you think I'd ever go near the pokies again?'

'May thinks you have.'

'I know.' He groaned again. 'And I let her believe...'

'Why?'

'I had a windfall,' he told them. At the look on Harry's face he shook his head. 'No. Not the kind you're thinking. My dad's been watching me...he was so upset when I got into the mess, but he wouldn't lift a finger to help us. I asked him but he wouldn't. ''You'll just gamble it away,'' he told me, and maybe he was right at that.'

'So?'

'So he came good. It's been two years since I've touched anything to do with gambling and he came to see me one night when May was on night shift. He gave me a gift. A deposit on a house. Or almost. The way my credit rating is, I have to have almost half the value or they won't touch me. Anyway, I scraped up the rest. I've still got one credit card. I went to see a financial advisor and he reckoned it was fine to run it up for three months until settlement. He worked it all out for us. The payments. What I have to do. I just need to work a few hours' overtime every week and that money goes straight into the credit card. And then…in another six weeks we get possession. It's a house May has loved for years. I was going to surprise her. For our wedding anniversary I was going to hand her the keys.'

'But May thought…'

'She must have found my credit-card statement,' Tom said heavily. 'She knew I was working overtime but there was no extra money coming in. And money going out—lawyers' fees and things—that I couldn't explain. I told her I was planning a surprise but she didn't believe me. She didn't trust… And I was so angry… Hell, I wanted her to trust me again. I wanted it so much. So I wouldn't tell her and she just said nothing—just started frantically trying to pay it off. And I was so damned stubborn I let her. And now this.'

Harry sat back on his heels. He stared at the man before him long and hard. Finally he said simply, 'What house?'

'The Maynard place.'

'Right.' Harry nodded, and Lizzie could see his mind in overdrive. 'This is what you're going to do.'

'What?'

'May's mum and dad are here now. They'll stay with her while she comes around, but for the next hour she's going to be so groggy that she won't take anything in. Meanwhile, I want you to find Neil Shannon. Urgently.'

'Neil… The photographer?'

'That's the one. He can do good work and he can move fast. You've got an hour—the pair of you. By the time May wakes up properly I want a poster-sized picture of that house right in front of her eyes.'

'But…a poster-sized…'

'Don't tell me you can't do it,' Harry said sternly. 'You've stuffed it. Now you need to fix it.'

'She should have trusted me.'

'She didn't walk out on you when most women would have,' Harry told him, his voice still stern. 'She didn't abandon you. She simply worked her guts out to try and fix your mess. She forgave you. Are you saying you're not going to forgive her now?'

'I don't—'

'Tom, you lost her house. She had to sell her beloved horses. She lost her respect in the community. To be honest, surprises aren't things she's going to want any more. Ever. She needs total and complete honesty from you, and she's going to need it for the rest of your lives. You've got a great woman. You nearly lost her—twice—but you have another chance. Don't stuff it yet again.'

Tom thought about it. And thought about it for a bit longer. And his lined face crumpled still more.

'I've been a fool,' he said at last, and Harry nodded. He wasn't in the mood for leniency.

'You have.'

'You're sure she's going to be OK?'

'I'm sure.'

'Well.' Tom rose on legs that seemed decidedly shaky. 'Well... Maybe I'd better go and organise a photograph, then.'

*   *   *

Lizzie had slivers of glass in her fingers. If she could have, she would have taken them out herself, but operating on her right hand with her left was impossible. She waited until Harry had talked to May's mum and dad and three kids, and then did a round of the little hospital's patients, all of whom were deeply upset by the afternoon's events. If he wondered why she didn't offer to help, he didn't say so—indeed, she had the impression that he'd have told her she wasn't wanted. She made her way back to the doctor's quarters and hugged Phoebe, drawing comfort from the big dog's placid and dopey presence.

'I love you, Phoeb,' she murmured, and felt like weeping. The big dog slurped her tongue down Lizzie's face and looked as if she agreed entirely. She was a very weepy kind of dog.

She was still there when Harry returned, sitting on the floor, hugging her dog, and Harry stopped at the sight of her.

'Are you OK?' he asked.

'F-fine.' The tables had turned, she thought. For the last three weeks he'd taken a back seat to her. She'd been the doctor and he'd—mostly—let her take the lead while his leg healed. But now there was no way he was taking a back seat. He might be wearing a cast, but he was very much a man in charge of his world.

That was what she wanted him to be. Not a patient. No way!

'It could have been so much worse,' he told her, kneeling down before her.

'Y-yes.'

'Lizzie, it's OK. She's fine.'

'I shouldn't care,' she said, hugging her dog like Phoebe was the only thing between her and madness. 'I shouldn't. And I do, so much. I can't bear it. If anything happens to May... To Lilly or May or Mavis with her blasted axe...'

'You know you'd get over it.'

'But I shouldn't care.'

'Why shouldn't you care?'

'Because it hurts,' she said miserably. And then she looked down at her hands. 'Like my fingers...'

'Your fingers.' He followed her gaze and his face snapped into a frown. 'Hell! Lizzie, why didn't you say?'

'We were a bit busy, if you'll remember,' she said dully.

'OK.' Harry's voice gentled still further and it was as much as Lizzie could do not to crumple right there. 'Sorry, Phoebe, but you need to get off your mistress's knee. She needs a doctor.'

He had the gentlest hands.

She sat in his room and watched as he gently probed every inch of her fingers. One, two, three slivers of glass... They'd been hurting badly but she'd hardly noticed. The pain in her heart was greater than the pain in her hands.

Because she knew now what she had to do.

'You know when you asked me to stay and work here?' she whispered as he bathed her hands with antiseptic and placed dressings over the deepest of the puncture wounds.

'Yes?' He looked up at her, with that smile that made her heart do back-flips. Only it had no business doing back-flips. He belonged to Emily. He belonged to Birrini. His smiles were not for her.

'I've decided I do want to be a family doctor,' she told him. 'I saw it today. I love what you do here. I love the way the community cares for each other. This life...it's what I want. I tried so hard not to care. I've been trying to be the ultimate professional—to not get involved in people's lives. But it hasn't worked. One locum with one caring doctor and it all slams back— what I loved about country practice. Why I wanted to be a doctor in the first place. You don't have to convince me to be a family doctor, Harry McKay. It's what I've always wanted. I just…lost courage for a while.'

'Then you'll stay?' It was like the sun coming out—the way he smiled. The way his eyes lit up.

It was so darned tempting.

But that was the way of madness and she knew it. She might be a family doctor, but not here. No!

'No, Harry, I can't stay.'

Silence. 'Why not?'

But he knew the answer. She read it in his face. He knew what she was going to say, but she knew before she gave her reasons out loud that no matter what she said—no matter what her reasons—he wasn't going to do one thing about it.

He couldn't. It was her problem, not his, and she knew that, too. But she said it anyway. It was embedded in her heart, and there was no way she could hide it. Not from herself. Not from him. Maybe not from anyone. The only thing she could do was finish her work here and leave.

But first it had to be said.

'Because I don't just love Birrini and the community here and the work,' she whispered, her eyes not leaving his face. Hoping against hope. 'I love you, as well as everyone else I've met in this crazy, gorgeous little town. But that's the problem. You see, Harry, the real problem is that it's you that I love the most of all.' Then, as he closed his eyes and she saw the shuttered look slam over his face, she shook her head. 'Harry, this isn't fair. It's not fair to land this on you and I'm expecting nothing. I know you're engaged to Emily. I know you don't want this. But it's there. I'm sorry, Harry, but there it is, and now you know why I have to leave.'

She'd known that he wouldn't do anything with it but this was awful. The night stretched before them. They had to eat together. They had to share a kitchen. But there was nothing to say that wasn't loaded.

'You're engaged to Edward,' he said at some time over a desultory dinner, and his voice was almost desperate.

'No.'

'You're not engaged?'

'No.'

'You lied?'

'I guess. Sort of.' She looked up at him, her face bleak. 'Edward asked me to marry him before I came down to Grandma's funeral. I didn't answer. I couldn't. Edward and I have been an item for ever. On and off. He keeps wanting to get married and I keep thinking I should. It's the sensible thing to do, but I can't. That's why I used the excuse of Phoebe's pregnancy to stay here longer. To give me breathing space. To think.'

'So you'll go back and marry him now?'

'What do you think?' she said on a note of anger. 'Of course I won't. Did you take in anything I just said?'

'Lizzie, I wouldn't interfere—'

'You already have. Leave it, Harry. If you can't go and stay in your wedding house that's waiting for you then stay here, but don't give me grief. Let's keep it formal from this moment on.'

Lizzie lay in her bed that night and she'd never felt so bleak in her life. Phoebe lay right on top of her. Usually she heaved the big dog off. She was so heavily pregnant that she weighed a ton—all right, she weighed a ton even when she wasn't pregnant—but tonight she was the only comfort Lizzie had.

Why on earth had she told Harry that she loved him?

He hadn't wanted it. She'd watched his face and it had shuttered so fast that she couldn't begin to imagine that she'd ever get close. He hadn't wanted her declaration, and why should he? He was engaged to be married to Emily. Sure, he had a fear of bridesmaids, but he'd never given her the slightest reason to think he didn't want to marry Em herself.

'He kissed me. He kissed me, Phoebe, and I've never been kissed like that. And the whole town was watching.'

Maybe men kissed like that…

'That's crazy, Phoeb. I've been solidly kissed in my time and there's never been the least suggestion in my head that my toes would drop off.' Which was what it had felt like when Harry had kissed her.

So maybe it hadn't felt like that for him?

It couldn't have.

She didn't have the first idea what he was thinking, she told herself as she huddled into her pillow. Not one idea in the world. She didn't know the man.

So how could she love him?

And what had she done in telling him? What damage? She'd thrown herself—and her pride—

straight at a man who was engaged to someone else, and both were in tatters now.

'You wouldn't debase yourself like that, would you, girl?' she asked Phoebe, and Phoebe opened her mouth wide and snored at a thousand or so decibels.

It was all the response a stupid question like that deserved.

'Why are you here?'

It was three in the morning. Harry was silently checking his patients. Not because he needed to—Isobel was on duty and she was extremely competent. She'd call him if he was needed. But still he walked the wards, limping slightly and leaning heavily on one crutch. He was better at walking than this, but he was tired. And where was sleep when a man needed it most?

In Ward Three May should have been asleep too, but as he opened her door she saw him and waved him weakly inside. Her face was swathed in bandages, she looked pallid and shocked, but her eyes were alert and awake. She even managed a slight smile of greeting.

'Are you in pain?' he asked, and she gave a faint shake of her head and then winced.

'Not much.'

He grinned, limping inside and crossing to the chair beside the bed. But he didn't sit. She needed to sleep, not socialise. 'You're lying,' he told her, and the smile behind her eyes deepened.

'Yeah, well.'

'I'll give you something.' He picked up her chart. 'According to this, you're overdue. A nice little cocktail of morphine and sedative. I'll fetch it now…'

'No, wait, Harry.' Her hand came out and caught his. She was weak with shock but there was still the hint of the laughter he was used to in her eyes. Just. 'You know what happened?'

'You had an argument with a tree. And lost. Anyone could have told you trees don't fight fair.'

'I was exhausted.' She shook her head, wincing again at the movement. That fractured cheek would have her wincing for a few weeks yet. 'I must have gone to sleep at the wheel, and it was so stupid. Did Tom tell you?'

'About the house.'

She nodded and turned her head painfully to the wall. There was Tom's poster—a picture of a beautiful timber cottage, with horses in the foreground and the river and bushland behind.

'He'd done it to surprise me,' she said bleakly. 'And I thought…I thought…'

'We all know what you thought. And no one's blaming you. He let you down so badly in the past that it was the natural thing to think.'

'But I love him,' she said distressfully. 'I hurt him. And now this…'

Harry hesitated and then covered her hand with his. 'I'm sure you'll find it in your hearts to start again.'

'Yeah? Like you can?'

'Sorry?'

'Melanie's death,' she whispered. 'Your dad's death. You've never let it go. Harry, I've been thinking…'

'Don't,' he said, startled.

'No, don't stop me.' She gripped his hand, trying to convey urgency. 'Harry, I've been watching you. For so long. You have no idea. All the time I've been hurting when Tom's been out of control, you've been hurting as well, but it's even worse. Because you don't have love underlying it. You didn't love Melanie. I saw you then. You were infatuated with glamorous and Melanie was surely glamorous. She was everything you thought you wanted in life, before you realised how shallow that sort of life was. And now…now you're doing it again.'

'I—'

But she was in no mood for interruptions. 'You don't love Emily either,' she said wearily. 'Don't tell me you do. And she doesn't love you. Emily's in love with the idea of being married to the town doctor. She's in love with the idea of weddings. But I would have married my Tom even if he'd had nothing—if he was nothing. You know what he said tonight? If I thought he was gambling again, why hadn't I just walked out? But he's a part of me. He hurts, I hurt. I love him so much. Like you love Lizzie.'

Silence. 'May, you need to go to sleep,' he said bleakly. 'I don't love Lizzie. I don't love…'

'Anyone?'

'I…'

'Start,' she whispered. 'Admit you and Emily are a mistake.'

'You need to be asleep.'

'And you need to be awake. I can't say this to you again after tonight. You're my boss. I work for you. Tomorrow I'll go back to being your patient and then a nurse in your hospital. But tonight…when I'm drugged out of my mind I can't be held responsible, I can say what I like. Lizzie and Phoebe…they light up this town. They light up your life. Don't mess with it, Dr

McKay.' She swallowed. 'There was this moment when I knew I was going to hit the tree... I thought...I thought I wasn't going to have anything any more. To be any more. That it was finished. And, you know, I don't think that I was angry with Tom. I thought...in that fleeting moment I thought that I hadn't had enough of my Tom. Of my boys. Of life. You take hold of it, Harry McKay, and stop being such a coward.'

'May...'

'OK, enough.' She bit her lip and smiled at him a little sheepishly as she finally released his hand. 'I've said what I've been wanting to say for years, and it was only seeing that damned tree in front of my nose that gave me the courage to say it. So don't wait for your own tree. And now...' She closed her eyes. 'Now maybe I could have that cocktail?'

Memo:

Ring vet and find out just what the gestation period for bassets really is.

Organise working life so we have two separate medical practices. Hers and mine.

Visit Emily's—no, not Emily's, Emily's and my—house and see if I can bear living with pink Chantilly lace.

Chantilly lace or Lizzie...

Breakfast was a very strained affair, interrupted by Emily. Harry's fiancée walked in when Harry had just bitten into his toast and marmalade, which he promptly dropped.

Emily stood at the back door, looking bright and breezy. She was wearing neatly fitted black trousers, a gorgeous white linen blouse and high white sandals. Her hair was swept up into a glamorous knot and she was wearing full make-up.

Lizzie was wearing faded pyjamas. She glanced up and thought, Emily.

Emily.

Why do I even bother? Why do I think about bothering? Sometimes there's no sense even competing.

She couldn't compete now—that was for sure. Luckily she was distracted, almost distracted enough not to register Emily's presence. She was stooping over Phoebe's basket. Phoebe had been restless in the night and Lizzie was worried about her. She tried not to look at Emily. She offered the big dog some toast, but Phoebe turned her nose away.

Trouble. If Phoebe wasn't eating, there were major problems.

'Hi, Emily,' she said, hardly looking up. 'Do you know anything about having puppies?'

But Emily wasn't looking at Lizzie. After one scorching glance at the pyjama-clad girl on the floor, she turned to her fiancé—who was looking particularly fetching himself in boxer shorts and white cast and nothing else.

'Are you living with Dr Darling?' Emily demanded, and Harry scratched his bare chest and appeared to think about it. It was maybe a bit hard to deny, seeing Harry was in his boxers and Lizzie was in her pyjamas. It *was* seven-thirty in the morning.

'What time did you arrive?' he asked, as Emily sat down. In front of Lizzie's toast. Lizzie thought about minding, but then decided she didn't. Or not very much.

How could you tell if a dog as fat as Phoebe was in labour? She put her hand on her belly, but there weren't any obvious contractions.

'I drove home late last night,' Emily was saying. 'My uncle rang me in Melbourne and said you'd be desperate for nurses. He said May's been hurt in a car accident.'

'She'll be OK.'

'So she was hurt?'

'A couple of fractures. Lacerations. She'll live.'

There wasn't a lot of warmth here, Lizzie thought. Ninety per cent of her attention was on her dog but she had enough left to lend an ear.

'You'll need me,' Emily said, and Harry nodded.

'We do.' And then, belatedly, like he'd just realised he hadn't said it, he added, 'We missed you.'

But Emily had moved on. There hadn't been a kiss, Lizzie thought. If she was Emily she'd have kissed Harry by now. Boy, would she have kissed him!

'Have you set the date for our wedding yet?' Emily was asking, and Lizzie turned her attention back to Phoebe. Maybe Emily was waiting until she wasn't here to get personal, she decided, and maybe she'd stay right where she was. She didn't want to think about Emily kissing Harry.

But they had their rights. They *were* engaged.

'I might just go and ring the vet,' Lizzie said. 'If you'll excuse me…'

Emily swivelled at that and stared down at her like she was some strange and foreign form of insect life. 'Why aren't you dressed?' she demanded.

'I'm in my pyjamas,' Lizzie said carefully. 'It's seven-thirty in the morning.'

'But Harry's not dressed either.'

Lizzie sighed. 'I haven't been in bed with your fiancé, if that's what you're implying,' she said tiredly. 'I've been in bed with a basset until her squirming drove me demented. Now, if you don't mind, I think we have a little obstetric emergency to cope with.'

'Do you reckon the puppies are coming?' Harry asked. He looked more interested in Phoebe than he was in Emily.

'I'm not sure.'

'I'll take a look.'

'Harry, we need to talk,' Emily snapped, and Harry nodded. Reluctantly.

'I guess we do.'

'Outside.'

'Fine.'

'I'll go and ring the vet,' Lizzie told them. She cast Phoebe another worried look but the big dog had her head down on her paws and looked more miserable than distressed. Early stages, Lizzie decided.

'Practise your breathing like we talked about,' she told Phoebe. 'I'll go and find us some help.'

The vet was succinct and reassuring. 'Don't fret. Unless she's clearly distressed, the best thing is to let her be. Tell you what. I'm going out to see a cow in labour now. That'll take me half an hour or so. What if I pop in and do a house call on Phoebe after that?'

'Would you? I don't like to think of bringing her down to your surgery.'

'Sure, of course I would.' She could hear Kim's grin down the phone. Kim was a young woman vet who Lizzie had decided early on could be a friend, and she knew the whole town was hanging out, waiting for these puppies. 'I understand your problem. If I had the choice of loading a cow into the back seat of your car and bringing her into surgery or loading Phoebe—maybe I'd choose the cow.'

That was all she could do for the moment for Phoebe. Phoebe seemed inclined to sleep, so Lizzie showered and dressed, trying rather self-consciously not to look any different from any other day. She decided finally to go really casual—just to show Emily she really didn't give a damn. Old jeans. Casual sweatshirt, with white coat thrown on over the top. No make-up. Then she checked on Phoebe who still seemed to want to sleep—maybe she wasn't in labour after all—and made her way over to the hospital. She may as well make herself useful while she waited for Kim's house call.

The hospital was quiet. May was deeply asleep. The bruising had coloured drastically in the night, leaving her face almost Technicolored. Tom was seated beside her, holding her hand.

'Have you been here all night?' she demanded, and he shook his head.

'Doc McKay made me go home. My parents are staying with the boys today, though, so I thought I'd stay with her a while.'

'You know she'll sleep.'

'I just want to be here,' Tom said in a cracked voice, his eyes not leaving May's.

Lizzie thought suddenly with a fierce ache in her heart, That's what I want. Some man to look at me when I'm black and blue and just love me...

No. Not some man.

Harry.

'Emily's back.' Lizzie was barely in Lilly's room before the teenager burst forth with her news. Word travelled fast in Birrini.

'Mmm.'

'So what are you going to do?'

'Read your chart and watch you eat a piece of toast.'

'No, but—'

'Eat,' Lizzie told her, and Lillian took a mouthful and swallowed almost at once, she was so eager to continue her train of thought.

'He can't marry Emily.'

'Why not?'

'He kissed you.'

'Yeah. Once. It hardly makes him unfaithful.'

'No…but he kissed you as if he meant it.'

'Eat.'

Another bite. 'You love him, don't you?'

'If I do, it's hardly your business.'

'I think you should fight Emily for him.'

'Oh, great. Pistols at dawn.'

There was a knock on the door and Lizzie turned away, almost in relief. A junior nurse stood there, clearly anxious.

'Yes, Terri?'

'There's someone at the nurses' station asking for you,' the girl said. 'I'll stay here with Lilly if you like.'

'Did someone say who someone was?' Lizzie asked.

'Just Edward. He said his name was Edward.'

CHAPTER TEN

THEY were all out there. In the nurses' station. Lizzie walked toward the group clustered in the entrance and she felt an overriding compulsion to turn and flee.

Doctors don't run from their problems, she told herself with something less than conviction. They face up to them.

And why would she want to flee from Edward?

Why indeed?

It really was Edward, all the way from Queensland. He was wearing one of the lovely Italian suits he'd had tailor-made in Milan last year. Edward was a very successful radiologist and he liked the world to acknowledge it. Just quietly. Indeed, if you'd accused him of smugness he'd have been horrified. Edward never boasted of his success, his privilege or his intelligence, all of which were extremely impressive. He was kind to people he perceived to be lesser beings and Lizzie had never been able to make him see that kindness itself was a form of being patronising.

So was patience, she thought. He'd been impressively patient with her and all it made her want to do was hit him.

'Lizzie,' he said, smiling as she made her way down the corridor toward him. He held out his hands. 'If the mountain won't come to Mohammed then Mohammed has decided he'd better come to the mountain.'

Oh, very oblique. She gave him a sickly smile. 'A mountain, huh. I'm not that fat. Go see Phoebe if we're talking about mountains.' But she gave him her hands and he pulled her close and kissed her while Harry and Emily looked on with interest.

'You didn't tell us you were engaged.' Emily was smiling her approval.

'I told Harry.' She collected herself and added, 'Not that I am.'

'I brought your ring with me,' Edward said, and she gave an inward groan.

'Edward—'

'When are you coming home?'

'The puppies haven't been born yet. Speaking of which—'

'We can transport them as soon as they're born. I talked to the airline.'

'*We* can't transport them anywhere. I've promised a puppy to one of the local children.

The puppy can't leave its mother for eight weeks.'

'Then we send the puppy back when it's ready,' Edward said with the patience he was famous for. 'Problem solved.'

'The puppies are due to be born any minute,' Emily said, brightening perceptibly with this lessening of a perceived threat. 'You could take all of them straight back to Queensland. Maybe even tomorrow.'

'She's my locum while we get married,' Harry said, and Emily arched her eyebrows and smiled.

'You haven't set another date. I vote we get another locum.'

'I like this one.'

'Harry…'

'I've got a broken leg.' Harry stuck it out in front of him like show and tell. 'I need help.'

'So we hire someone else,' Emily said.

'Lizzie really needs to come home.' Edward was back in patronising mode—already. Explaining things to someone who was a wee bit thick. 'I thought the dog was about to deliver her pups any minute or I'd never have allowed her to stay.'

'Hey,' Lizzie broke in, incensed. 'You'd never *allow* me—?'

'When are you getting married?' Emily asked, and Edward turned his full attention on Emily. Well, why not? You could see his reasoning in his face. Emily was looking exceedingly cute and Lizzie was looking a bit worse for wear. She'd never wear these clothes for Edward. He hated jeans. He hated sweatshirts.

But underneath…she was the same woman that he declared ten years ago he'd marry, and if there was one thing Edward didn't do it was change his mind.

'We'll be married as soon as Lizzie agrees to a date,' he told Emily. 'My mother has it all planned.'

'So has mine,' Emily told him, warming to the theme closest to her heart. 'Only Harry keeps being so difficult. I mean, if I have six bridesmaids then surely he can find six groomsmen.'

'Mine's the opposite problem.' Edward dug his hands in his pockets—Careful, Lizzie thought, you're spoiling the line of your suit— and flashed Lizzie a look of affection mixed with annoyance. 'Lizzie doesn't believe in bridesmaids.'

'You don't believe in bridesmaids?' Harry said, looking up sharply.

'All my friends hate chiffon,' Lizzie told him. She was feeling as if things were getting away from her here. She made a huge effort. She'd been going out with Edward since medical school. Off and on. His devotion should surely be rewarded. Maybe she should start thinking seriously of marriage. 'Maybe I could get Phoebe to carry the ring.'

'She'd eat it,' Harry said, and grinned.

It was the grin that did it every time. Right when she thought she had it together, out came that grin and she was lost.

There was no way she could marry Edward. Not when that grin existed in the world.

'I'm sorry...' she started, but there was another interruption. A woman, wearing stained overalls and Wellingtons, was standing at the hospital entrance, waving wildly. Kim. The vet.

And Lizzie's thoughts flew straight back to Phoebe. It had been half an hour since she'd checked her. She shouldn't have left. Kim had told her she'd go straight to the doctor's quarters to check. What was she doing here?

'What's happening?'

Kim was standing in the entrance, reluctant to bring her filthy boots into the antiseptically clean hospital. 'Didn't you tell me Phoebe's in your kitchen?' she called.

'Yes.'

'I just went to check. The doors are shut but she's not there. Her basket's gone as well. Have you moved her somewhere else?'

Lizzie turned to Harry. 'Did you…?'

But Harry was looking as puzzled as she was. 'She was asleep by the stove ten minutes ago.'

'It takes a crane to move her.' Lizzie shook her head. 'I need to—'

'Lizzie, we need to talk,' Edward said urgently, catching her arm, but she shrugged him off.

'Medicine comes first, Edward, you know that. It's the basis for our whole relationship. I have puppies to deliver—if I can find Phoebe. Talk to Emily about bridesmaids or something. Or how important it is to be a doctor's partner.'

'Liz…'

'I'm sorry.' She bit her lip, catching herself through her distress. 'That was unfair. I'm just worried about Phoebe. If you'll excuse me.'

And she left them staring after her as she headed for where her dog should have been.

She really was gone. Lizzie stared down at the corner by the stove where Phoebe had spent an ever-increasing amount of time over the past weeks. In those first days here the big basset had been frantic whenever Lizzie had left, as if somehow she'd sensed that Lizzie was her only contact with the beloved old lady who'd been her mistress. But gradually she'd settled. She liked Harry—she'd made that plain. She liked Lizzie. She liked the constant stream of locals who popped in to say hi and to Phoebe-sit. But gradually her girth had got the better of her and she'd subsided into her basket and watched the world with the increasingly introspective gaze of all expectant mums.

When Lizzie had lifted her off the bed in the middle of the night, she'd waddled out here. This morning Lizzie had looked at her and had thought Phoebe wouldn't move until the puppies were born.

So where was she?

'Maybe she's gone outside to find somewhere more private.' Kim was right behind her, sensing her fright. 'Lizzie, dogs often do that. They decide for themselves where they're going to pup.'

'I'd believe that,' Lizzie said, still staring at the corner, 'but she'd hardly have hauled her basket with her.'

Silence. There was a soft thud, thud behind them and Harry was right there. His crutch was making his arrival distinct.

'Where the hell—?'

'What have you done with Emily and Edward?' Lizzie demanded, momentarily distracted, and Harry shrugged.

'They're talking weddings. I think they've hit a vein. They've tapped into something more important than world hunger. Where's Phoebe?'

'She's gone,' Lizzie said blankly, but Harry was already looking closely at the kitchen floor. Then bending to look closer.

'The basket's been dragged out the door. Look.'

The floor was made of polished boards. The boards gathered dust fast and no one had swept that morning. The trail where something had been pulled across the floor was clearly visible and on the edge of the screen door a splinter had jagged the edge of the blue cotton basket, leaving a sliver of material still attached.

'Why would Phoebe drag her basket—?'

'She wouldn't,' Kim said. The vet was starting to look concerned. 'Not that I'm casting aspersions on your dog's intelligence, Lizzie, but to figure she'd go somewhere else to have the pups and think about taking her bed with her…that'd take at least two neurons.'

'Which is one more than Phoebe's got,' Harry added, but he wasn't smiling.

'So someone's dragged her basket...'

'With Phoebe in it, at a guess. I mean, otherwise they could just have picked up the basket.'

'I don't believe this,' Lizzie said faintly. 'Who'd steal a basset?'

They stared at each other uncomprehendingly.

'She's not even a pedigree,' Lizzie whispered. 'Grandma found her when she was six months old. She reckoned someone pushed her out of a moving car. No one wants Phoebe.'

'She's mostly basset,' Kim said. 'But that tail...there's something else there.'

'It's a cute tail,' Lizzie muttered, and Harry's arm was suddenly round her shoulders.

'It's a great tail. The fact that it'd look better on a Dalmatian is immaterial. Look, what have we got here? One lost dog? One stolen dog? Neither makes sense. My bet is that someone like Jim has come in and decided that Phoebe shouldn't be alone. They'll have taken her home to watch over her.'

Lizzie brightened. Harry being right beside her was enough to make any girl's mood lift, and what he was saying was sensible. Dognappers didn't make sense.

But... 'Jim wouldn't have dragged the basket,' she objected.

'If Phoebe wouldn't move and he wanted to shift her, I'd imagine he might well have dragged the basket. Do you imagine anyone carrying that dog further than he had to?'

'That'll be it,' Kim said, relieved. She glanced at her watch. 'Look, I'm having a bit of trouble here. My cow's had her calf but I need to go back and check on her again. I took a few minutes off to check on Phoebe but...'

'But if we can't find her—'

'I'll be back in half an hour,' Kim said. 'Or I'm on the end of a mobile phone. Call me if you need me.'

'I'll go and call Jim,' Harry said. The door had closed behind Kim, but Lizzie was still standing looking at the place where Phoebe's basket had been.

She shouldn't have left her.

It was ridiculous. She was being ridiculous. Jim had taken the dog to take care of her. She'd left her for half an hour and the vet had said it'd be OK. She wasn't irresponsible.

This was Grandma's dog. She'd cared for Grandma and therefore she was responsible for Grandma's dog.

No. It was more than that, she thought savagely. Responsibility didn't come into it any more.

It was Phoebe herself. Her great dopey basset with the Dalmatian tail. She'd tried so hard to stay dispassionate. She'd tried. It hadn't worked. She'd fallen for a great lumbering hound of a mutt. She'd fallen for a community.

She'd fallen for a doctor called Harry.

His hand was still on her shoulder and he was watching her, his eyes steady and warm and reassuring, and she wanted to turn into his shoulder and weep. She wanted to hold on and hold on and not let go.

No. She had Phoebe to worry about. Everything else had to be put on the back burner for now.

Or... Everything else had to be put on the back burner for ever.

She hauled herself away from him and she could only hope that he didn't guess what a Herculean task it was to step away from the warmth those arms promised.

'Find Jim,' she whispered. 'I'll have a look outside. Just in case.'

'Just in case your dog decided to take her bed outside for a bit of morning sun?'

'It's possible.'

'As I said, one neuron too few.'

'Criticise your own loved ones,' she muttered. 'Leave mine alone.'

And she walked out and slammed the door behind her.

She'd walked ten yards down the garden path before Amy found her. The little girl came flying along the cliff path, her pinched face white with shock. She cannoned straight into Lizzie before she saw her. Lizzie caught Amy's shoulders and set her back, steadying her, noting the tear-stained cheeks and the eyes wide with terror.

'Amy.'

It was one word, but it steadied her. The child stared up at her, mute.

'Amy,' Lizzie said again, more gently, and gathered the little girl into her. She was stooping, kneeling, cradling the child against her, and out it came, great whooping sobs that racked the slight body until it seemed she'd tear apart.

'Amy, no.' Lizzie gave her a hard squeeze and then put her away from her, holding her at arm's length. She took off the child's glasses, wiped them and popped them on again. 'Stop this. You need to pull yourself together to tell me.'

'They can't... They'll kill... She's gone over... Phoebe...'

Lizzie's heart clenched within her. But somehow she kept her face impassive, her voice stern.

'They'll kill who?'

'They took Phoebe. Kylie and Rose. They thought it was really funny. They hauled her into the back of Kylie's brother's billy-cart and they hauled her along the cliff. They were going to stick her in the cave. Hide her. Just...just 'cos everyone's been making a fuss of the pups and I'm having one.'

'They told you this?'

'Kylie's brother told me. He's in my class and I knew they were doing something. They were giggling all yesterday and writing notes. Billy's not bad. They're mean to him, too. So I asked him and he told me and I followed. They're bigger than me and I thought...I thought I'd just watch and see where they took her. But she was too big. They hauled her into the billy-cart and she was really heavy and they pulled it along the cliff and then as it turned a corner and started to go downhill it sort of lurched and Rose let it go and...'

'And...' Lizzie was feeling sick.

'And it rolled over the edge of the cliff and smashed on the rocks below. She's lying there. Kylie and Rose ran away and I came... I can't get down there. I can see her and... Oh, Dr Darling, I think she's dead.'

Big breath.

Another big breath.

Do not panic, Lizzie. Do not...

'Where on the cliff?' she asked.

'Up there.' Amy pointed to the headland. 'Where it turns. If you look down you can see.'

'You've found me. You've done really well,' she told Amy. 'It's up to me now. Go into the hospital and tell any of the nurses—or Dr McKay—what's happened. Tell them to call the vet. Run.'

Lizzie stared down the cliff face. Here the beach was unapproachable except by boat. But Phoebe wasn't on the beach. She was about fifteen feet down the cliff face and there was a drop of another ten feet to the sea.

The cliff wasn't sheer but it sloped at a frightening angle. Phoebe wouldn't have dropped straight down. There were skid marks on the path. Here the path dipped and turned and it was easy to see what had happened. With the dead weight of Phoebe inside, the cart had lurched out of control and run over the edge. It must have crashed down onto the ledge. There were a couple of wheels lying on the ledge, but Lizzie could see timber from the remains of the cart crashing about in the waves below.

And Phoebe.

Like the wheels, she remained on the ledge. She was a huge liverish blob, unmoving.

'Phoebe,' Lizzie yelled, but the dog didn't move.

Phoebe…

It was all too much. Phoebe. Grandma.

Harry.

They were all caught up in her mind. Four weeks ago she'd been Dr Darling, independent career-woman. Now… Her grandmother's death had smashed the first layer of her armour. It had made her see she wasn't invincible. And now she stood on the top of the cliff and she knew exactly what she was going to do.

Something really, really foolish.

It was crazy.

She did it anyway.

She sat down on her backside, she said a silent prayer to whoever looked after pregnant bassets and really stupid doctors and slid over the edge.

As big dippers went, it was a beauty. The surface was loose shale. Lizzie was wearing tough jeans and they acted as a buffer, but once she was over the edge there was no stopping.

She hurtled downwards, fiercely balancing, aiming to one side of Phoebe so she wouldn't squash what was left of her dog.

'Oweee…' Where the squeal came from she had no idea—a kid on a big dipper had nothing on her.

And somehow she did it. She hit the ledge. Her legs shot out in front of her and hit the slight rise before the ledge gave way to the drop to the sea, and she sprawled to an ignominious halt.

Ouch.

She lay winded and looked up at the sky.

She was still alive.

Good. Great. She felt a few limbs and tried a few breaths just to see if they'd work and, magic of magic, they did. There was a bit of pain in the seat of her jeans but, hey, that was nothing. Gravel rash?

Phoebe.

She slid around and thought, Whoops, maybe gravel rash has a downside. But she was a doctor. She had a patient to attend to. Triage. Gravel rash could wait.

Phoebe was alive.

She wasn't stirring. She lay on her side, her flanks heaving. Her one visible eye looked up at Lizzie, desperate, and Lizzie found herself cradling the big dog, holding her close and...yep, she was crying. Good professional technique, Dr Darling. Sob all over the patient first thing!

What damage?

She hauled herself back and made herself turn into a doctor—sort of.

Phoebe didn't even have gravel rash.

What the...?

She ran her hands over the dog's big body, lifting—well, heaving—following the folds of flab. Nothing.

Not a scratch.

She'd come down in the cart. She'd been thrown out and the cart had smashed, but Phoebe herself was unscratched.

But why wasn't she moving?

The puppies...

Phoebe's eyes were almost speaking. She whimpered and whimpered again.

'What's wrong? What's wrong, girl?'

Phoebe was straining. As Lizzie watched, a spasm seemed to shake her and a tremor ran through the big body. Another whimper.

How long? How long had she been straining? Lizzie had read up in her dog books. Second-stage labour in bitches took at most about half an hour. If things were going wrong…

'Lizzie?'

She looked up, and there was Harry. He was standing at the top of the cliff and his voice sounded desperate. 'Lizzie!'

'I'm down here,' she called, and she could almost see him sag with relief.

'I can see that you're down there,' he said carefully, with what seemed almost superhuman restraint. 'Very good. Very informative. How the hell did you get there?'

'I slid.'

'You slid.'

'On my backside.'

She turned back to Phoebe who was moaning and heaving again.

'I think she's in trouble,' she called. 'I think the puppies are coming but they might be stuck.'

'Lizzie…'

'Mmm?' She was concentrating on Phoebe.

There was silence from the top of the cliff. Harry seemed to be having trouble taking things in.

Finally he asked, 'Is she hurt, apart from the puppies?'

'No. I don't think so.'

'That figures,' he said. 'With that fat.'

'That's right. In time of crisis insult the patients.'

'Are you aware of the risks you took?'

'Fetch Kim.'

'Stay there,' he ordered.

'Yeah, right. Where do you think I'm going?'

But he was gone.

Where were the puppies? How far away?

How dilated did dogs' cervixes get? Lizzie wondered. This one looked ready to go. Phoebe was straining. Why wasn't anything happening? Had she been hurt in the fall? Internal injuries? What—?

'Move over.'

She stared up. Harry was at the top of the cliff. He had a backpack on and he was holding a rope.

'You can't.' She was on her feet. 'Are you mad? You've got a broken leg.'

'And you could have broken your neck. I have a rope. Attached to a tree. I've been a rock-climber in my time, Liz. There's only one damned fool in this picture and that's you.'

'You can't,' she repeated. 'Harry, your leg…'

'Move,' he ordered, and slipped over the edge of the cliff and came down to reach her.

He had indeed done rock-climbing. The way he slid down the rock-face was nothing short of amazing. He was controlled every step of the way—he'd fastened his rope to a tree and was belaying, or whatever rock climbers called it, but he looked thoroughly professional—even if he did have a leg in plaster.

He looked wonderful, Lizzie thought. Just wonderful. And when he landed beside her it was all she could do not to grab him and hold him and...

She didn't need to. He grabbed her and held her and put his face in her hair and started swearing. Over and over and over.

She didn't care. She could feel his heartbeat. If this was what it took to get him here, then...

Phoebe.

'Um...Phoebe,' she murmured, and he hauled her in closer.

'Have you any idea what I thought when I heard you scream?'

'I love you,' she said tangentially.

'I thought you were dead.'

'I love you lots.'

'I'll wring your neck. If ever you do anything so damned stupid again...'

He loved her. She could feel it. He just had to stop swearing and admit it.

But they did have a patient in labour.

'Phoebe,' she tried again, and this time he heard. He sighed, held Lizzie away from him—with real reluctance—and turned to look down at the dog.

'She's in trouble?'

'She's panting. She's been straining. She doesn't look hurt but, oh, Harry...'

'Dogs always pant in labour.'

'How do you know?'

He grinned and pointed to the phone on his belt. 'I rang Kim. While I ran here. Until I heard you scream. She's probably still on the end of the line.'

She wasn't. Nor was she when they tried to contact her again.

'She was out in the middle of a paddock when I called,' Harry said, running his hands over Phoebe's flank. 'She said she'd come straight away. The reception's awful between here and the farm she's been working on.'

'So do we wait?'

They were stooped over Phoebe. Harry had sat, his plastered leg before him.

'I should scrub,' he said, and Lizzie looked startled.

'Scrub?'

'She's a big dog. They'll be big puppies. I don't see why the logistics shouldn't be the same as for people.' He hesitated. 'If I use surgical gloves they'll be antiseptic enough. And lubricant.'

'You brought those things with you?'

'Of course I did,' he told her, trying not to sound smug—but he looked smug.

'You're in for it now,' she told him. 'Really in for it.'

'Why?' He was pulling his gloves from the backpack.

And there was nothing to tell him but the truth.

'Harry McKay, if you've brought surgical gloves and lubricant down this cliff to save my puppies then I intend to marry you. I'm sorry, but there it is. You don't marry me, I'm abducting you. Em doesn't stand a snowball's chance in a bushfire.'

'Neither does Edward,' he told her, but before she had a chance to respond to that, he became intent on what he was doing with Phoebe.

Silence.

'I think...' He frowned. 'I'm not sure what I'm feeling but it seems as if there's one stuck. She's straining against it.'

'Can you…?'

'I need more lubricant.'

She handed it to him. It was like an operating theatre—the world's weirdest operating theatre.

She was kneeling, her face intent. 'What—?'

'Shh.'

She shushed.

Phoebe gave a long, low moan and shuddered again, and Harry winced. 'They're some contractions.'

'Can you shift…?'

'I think… Wait…'

'Don't push, Phoeb,' Lizzie said, holding the big dog's head. 'Pant.'

Phoebe stared up at her—and panted.

'Hey!' It was an exclamation of surprise from Harry. 'Hey…'

'What?'

'It's moving.'

And ten seconds later the first of Phoebe's eight puppies slid out into Harry's waiting hands.

Memo:

Must remember what it is to be professional after delivery.

Must remember…what?

Must remember this moment for ever.

The puppies were wonderful. As they cleared the membranes from each perfect little nose and Lizzie handed the puppies to Phoebe to be licked and inspected and gathered to the maternal bosom, she thought she'd never seen anything so wonderful in her whole life.

'They look like golden retrievers,' Harry said, as the last puppy settled with his mother. Harry's voice was distinctly unsteady. 'Mixed with basset. And there's definitely a spot of Dalmatian in there as well.'

'They're wonderful,' Lizzie murmured, her voice laced with tears.

'Lizzie?'

She looked up at him, her eyes shining.

'Mmm.'

'They're not as wonderful as you,' he said softly, and she shook her head.

'Nope. It's you who's wonderful.'

'Want to make it a competition?'

'I might,' she said cautiously.

'Tell you what,' he said, gathering her into his arms and holding her with such infinite tenderness that the world shifted and shifted again, and when it had settled it was right where it was meant to be. Right where it had been intended to be all along.

'Wh-what…?'

'It's a kissing competition,' he told her. 'I'll kiss you. You kiss me back. And we'll keep on kissing until we've finally figured who's more wonderful than who.'

'It'll never work.' She was holding him tight, her love, her life, her future.

'What'll never work?' He was temporarily distracted. Or maybe he was permanently distracted. From this day forth...

'The competition.'

'Oh, that. No sweat. We just keep kissing until it does.'

Only, of course, it couldn't last. Amy had collected everyone in the hospital, and when they finally broke apart half the world was standing on the cliff path peering down at them with various levels of incredulity.

'Harry!' Emily was saying in tones of outrage.

'Elizabeth!' Edward was right beside her with outrage, and the two stood together in an unconscious union of affronted dignity.

'I thought she was dead,' Harry said, in a dazed sort of been-kissed-very-soundly voice to no one in particular. 'When she yelled.' He might have ceased kissing Lizzie but he wasn't letting her go. 'For a minute there I thought I'd lost her.' He looked ruefully up at his erstwhile fiancée. 'I'm sorry, Emily, but I'm marrying Lizzie.'

'You're marrying Lizzie?' It was Lillian, staring over the edge in stunned delight. She was holding Amy by one hand, and Joey had hold of the other. A group. A little family all of its own.

'I'm marrying Lizzie,' Harry repeated, and he turned back to Lizzie. 'I'm sorry, Em, but there it is.'

'But…what about my bridesmaids?'

'This is appalling,' Edward managed. 'To treat a woman like this.' Unconsciously his hand came out to grip Emily's. Emily did that to men. She was like a piece of Dresden china, perfectly executed and delicate. In need of protection.

In need of a radiologist…

'I don't… I can't…'

Edward's arm came around her waist.

'But the puppies…'

It was Amy again, her ashen face trying to focus through her thick smeared-again glasses.

'We have eight gorgeous puppies.' Lizzie held one up. 'Eight. Eight fabulous, wonderful puppies for you to choose from, Amy.'

'A boat's on its way to pick you up from the bottom.' It was Kim, shoving her way to the front. 'You're sure you guys are all OK?'

'One mother, eight babies and two obstetricians, all accounted for,' Harry said, and hauled Lizzie in to kiss her again.

'Um…would you mind refraining just for a moment?' Kim asked.

Harry grinned and nodded and let Lizzie go. About two inches. 'Yes, Doctor.'

'The puppies are well?' Kim asked, and Harry nodded.

'All well.'

'I don't want one as a mascot,' Joey called. 'I want one for real.'

'And I need one, too,' Lillian said. 'Please…'

'Me, too.' It was Terry, who'd come in today for his check-up and had somehow been drawn in to the excitement. His mother was standing by his side. 'Mum, my testicles hurt a whole heap before Dr McKay operated. You said if I was good… You said if I didn't tell the other kids what had happened to me, you'd get me a present. Mum, a puppy'd be great. I could call him…Nuts!'

Her son, talking about testicles in public! Lizzie looked up at the woman's face and choked with laughter. Amazingly, Terry's mother's puritanical sternness was threatening to crack apart, right there and then. There was laughter on the woman's face. And…the beginnings of joy?

Who could not smile at this happy ending? At this happy beginning. A puppy called Nuts. The world was changing in all sorts of wonderful ways.

'And me.' It was Tom, May's big husband. Heavens, the whole hospital must be on the cliff-top. 'May and I have a property to fill with animals. One of those puppies would fit right in.'

'They do look cute.' It was Emily. From the sanctuary of Edward's protective arm she'd sniffed herself back under control and now she was peering down the cliff to where Harry had lifted a pup who'd squirmed his way out of range of his mother's licks.

'I'll buy one for you,' Edward said, astonishing even himself. He coughed and tried to glare but his arm tightened on Emily. 'How much?'

Emily gazed up at him, amazed. There was a moment's stunned silence at this unexpected turn of events. Then, while they watched, Emily's face changed. She smiled. And she moved imperceptibly closer while Edward's arm hauled her even nearer.

'How much?' Edward asked.

'We'll have to see.' Harry's grin was threatening to split his face. 'Dr Darling and I need to discuss it. At leisure. Put in your bids and we'll think about it. But you can't have them all.'

'Why not?' Amy was smiling and smiling. And smiling some more. She'd thought Phoebe was dead. She'd thought the end of the world had come. Now she knew one of these puppies was definitely hers. She'd saved Phoebe. The little girl was growing in stature while they watched. 'Why can't everyone have one?'

'Lizzie and I want one,' Harry said. And then he looked down at the squirming mass of brand-new puppies. 'Or maybe two.'

'And no one gets a single puppy until after the wedding,' Lizzie decreed.

The wedding?

Harry looked tenderly at his love, and the look on his face said he knew exactly what wedding she was talking about. Whose wedding. His arm tightened around her and all the joy of the morning was in his face. 'Why not?' he asked tenderly. 'Why not, my love?'

'Because I don't want bridesmaids,' she managed. 'Instead of bridesmaids, I want brides-pups. Eight brides-pups with Phoebe as matron of honour.'

Memo:
Real doctors don't tie pew ribbons.
Real doctors tie...basset ribbons?
Nine basset ribbons. Not enough, really.
Maybe we could aim for more.